I0690181

AN ANTHOLOGY OF EROTICA

Gay Love Stories

First Edition

Published by The Nazca Plains Corporation
Las Vegas, Nevada
2009

ISBN: 978-1-935509-24-0

Published by

The Nazca Plains Corporation ®
4640 Paradise Rd, Suite 141
Las Vegas NV 89109-8000

PUBLISHER'S NOTE
An Anthology of Erotica - Gay Love Stories is a work of fiction created wholly by *Hank Brooks'* imagination. All characters are fictional and any resemblance to any persons living or deceased is purely by accident. No portion of this book reflects any real person or events.

Cover, Frenk Kaufmann
Art Director, Blake Stephens

DEDICATION

To Leo, who allows me the time to write my stories

AN ANTHOLOGY OF EROTICA

Gay Love Stories

First Edition

Hank Brooks

CONTENTS

ALONG CAME ANTONIO

Gino sat at the same table for at least two hours every afternoon, at the outdoor café right across the street from his apartment. The street on which the café was located was notorious for being a cruising area for the city's gay young men. You can keep April in Paris. Gino could not get enough of April in Rome. The young men who passed his table were candy for Gino's poor old eyes. Their tight trousers accentuated their bubble butts and ample packages, and made Gino's mouth water.

At seventy years young, Gino could easily get himself off with his semi-hard dick, but he had no illusions that he could ever snare one of the beauties who passed daily by his table, nor did he ever try. Some of them had become aware that he was a fixture in the neighborhood. They would stop for a quick, "Good afternoon," and "How are you doing old man?" Gino would not answer, but he would smile and wave at the young men.

Gino's expectations were not high. Six years ago he lost his partner and companion of over fifty years. He was a sad and lonely old man. His dreams were simple. All he wanted was to meet another man of any age, but preferably a senior citizen. He needed someone to be with, and to talk to, and to go to the movies with, and to share his meals with. Most of all he needed someone to lie with him in his bed at night. He needed someone who would hold him in his arms and whom he could hold in his arms. He so missed holding a naked man and fondling him, and kissing him, and running his hands up and down his back. The yearning was so great that he could feel the hurt throughout his whole body, so every day he sat at his table and admired the young men and ached for a companion.

One day, a gentleman, about Gino's age, sat down at the table next to Gino. He ordered a cappuccino and nursed it for about two hours before he left. During that time he too seemed to be admiring and staring at the rear ends of the young studs who passed by.

The next day, moments after Gino sat down at his table, the same gentleman sat down at the one next to him again. This time when he seated himself, he nodded slightly at Gino, who politely nodded back. The waiter took both their orders before retreating inside the restaurant. He was back in a few minutes with espressos for each of them. When the gentleman raised his cup, he said to Gino, "Salute".

"Salute," Gino responded and raised his cup. Then they sat in silence and enjoyed the scenery.

On the third day, they greeted each other with a smile. About a half hour into their viewing, the gentleman said to Gino quite unexpectedly, "Oh how I wish I were fifty years younger. That one that just passed by has a killer ass. I'd give anything to caress it."

"Me too," Gino agreed, but said not another word. "Well," he thought, still without any expectations, "the man is gay and very good looking."

The greetings and the once in awhile comments continued for more than three weeks. Finally one day, the other man said to Gino, "Signor, I feel as if we are getting to be old acquaintances." He stuck out his hand and introduced himself, "My name is Antonio."

Gino could not believe the man's audacity. He was very shy by nature and a very private person, but at the same time, he was not impolite. He extended his hand, shook the gentleman's hand and said, "My name is Gino." Now that they were properly introduced, they became less formal. Even Gino mellowed out a bit. Now when a particularly beautiful ass passed by, the two discussed the merits of it and laughed at their observations and their jokes. Their conversations were limited to comments regarding the eye candy which passed them by.

They were in the middle of the sixth week of their 'relationship' when Antonio dared to ask Gino, "Do you ever miss not going to work? Do you miss not having a place to go and having a purpose?"

Gino smiled at Antonio, and took a moment before he answered. "Yes," he finally said, "but only because I am so lonely. If I had a friend to share my remaining years with, I guess I wouldn't miss it at all."

"I feel the same way," Antonio said.

After that they sat in silence until eventually Antonio got up and nodded goodbye. "Ciao," he said as he left for the day.

Gino did not see Antonio for nearly two weeks after that. As flimsy as their friendship was, Gino realized that he missed Antonio terribly. He was shocked at his own feelings. He admonished himself for not having asked Antonio for his telephone number for just such a situation. He began to imagine and fear all sorts of scenarios. Perhaps Antonio had died, or worse, perhaps he was very ill and had no one to look after him. When the thought that Antonio might be ill came to him, he began to get teary eyed.

But in the end there was nothing he could do. He certainly could not call everyone in the phone book with the name Antonio. And what if he was just listed as 'A. Something or other?' He did reason that Antonio lived nearby and that would limit his search if he really dared to do such a thing, which was highly unlikely. He just resigned himself to the fact that Antonio was gone.

Then one day he looked up to see Antonio approaching the café. He looked well enough but somewhat pale. In a manner totally uncharacteristic of him, Gino jumped up to greet Antonio. "Where have you been, Antonio? I missed you."

"I've just had a terrible battle with the flu, but I'm feeling much better now. How are you my friend?"

"I'm fine. I'm fine," Gino answered and without thinking about it he pointed to the vacant seat at his table, and he said to Antonio, "Here sit with me."

The June air was warm and balmy, but they ordered hot cappuccino anyway. "Do you live alone?" Gino inquired.

"Sadly, yes. I had to rely on my landlady for assistance," Antonio answered lowering his head.

"I live alone too," Gino said smiling. "Would it be alright with you if we exchanged telephone numbers? This way, if one of us becomes ill again, he can inform the other, and perhaps be of assistance. I truly feared that the worst had happened to you."

Unexpectedly Antonio laid his hand on top of Gino's. "How kind of you," he said.

When Antonio's hand touched him, Gino became overwhelmed with emotion. Nobody had touched him in such a kind and loving manner in better than six years. He had to hold back tears and he allowed his other hand to rest on top of Antonio's. As he did that their eyes met and they smiled at one another. Antonio's smile reacted on Gino as a slight tingle in his long dormant groin. He wondered if the same was happening to Antonio.

Antonio pulled his hand away and took his wallet from his pocket. He removed a card from the wallet and gave it to Gino, who looked at the card and smiled. "You live right around the corner," he said.

"Yes," Antonio said. "I moved there just a couple of weeks before I first saw you at this café."

Gino reached into his wallet, and removed his card and gave it to Antonio. As he did so, he said to Antonio, "I am so glad we've met."

"I am too."

They resumed sipping their cappuccino and commenting on the passing parade. When it was about time to go, neither seemed to want to be the first to leave so Antonio finally dropped his guard and said, "Gino, my friend. Would you honor me by having dinner with me tonight? My treat."

Gino laughed. "Are you asking me out on a date? Because if you are, the answer is, yes."

Antonio laughed and took Gino's hand again. "I guess I am," he said.

They arranged to meet at seven at a ristorante they both knew which was just a street away. All the while they were making plans for the evening, Antonio had been holding Gino's hand. When he got up to leave, he kissed the back of Gino's hand. Antonio may have kissed Gino's hand, but he pierced Gino's heart. The feel of that kiss almost made Gino swoon.

At home Gino was beside himself with excitement. He showered and when he was dry he poured talc generously over his body to avoid any odor of sweat. He shaved and used too much after shave. He wore his best shirt and gabardine trousers with his very best black leather shoes. When he was all spiffy and ready to go, he realized that he had an hour and a half to go before meeting Antonio. He sat down quietly in his reclining chair, placed his hands in his lap and waited for the time to pass.

When Gino arrived at the restaurant ten minutes early, Antonio was already there waiting for him. He was sitting on a bench outside the entrance. He jumped up when he saw Gino and instinctively, the two men embraced and kissed each other very chastely on both cheeks.

When they entered the restaurant, Antonio looked around and asked to be seated at a quiet corner table which was available. He ordered the wine and told the waiter he would order their meal after they had finished their first glass.

They were relatively quiet at first and then Antonio started to tell Gino about his past life with his late beloved partner, who was gone three years now.

"I met Pierre when I was fifteen. His family was French and his father came from France to teach French at our high school. His father was obese and his shirt buttons were always popping open. Furthermore, he spoke Italian with a very thick French accent which was difficult to decipher. One day in the school yard I was making fun of the teacher when out of nowhere I received a jab across my jaw, and I fell to the ground. 'That's my father you're talking about,' Pierre screamed at me.

"Of course, he was instantly sorry and he helped me back on my feet and took me to the boy's wash room to help me clean up and wash my face. I had a bruise on my chin for days, but I didn't care. I was already in love with Pierre. He offered to make up for his violent action by buying me a gelato after school. Naturally I accepted. We became the best of friends and then lovers. Now don't laugh at me, but Pierre was the only man I was ever intimate with."

"Why would I laugh? Jacob was the only man I have ever been intimate with. Strangely I met him in the school yard too. We were in elementary school. Jacob was a Jew. His father was a dentist who had survived the holocaust. Not withstanding the fact that Dr. Sartori was the best dentist in Rome, and everyone in the neighborhood used his services, the boys in the school yard were taunting Jacob and calling him 'Christ killer.' Jacob was in tears.

"Now I was always big for my age. I shooed the other boys away and took Jacob under my wing. Every day after school, either he was at my house or I was at his. Mostly we were alone in our houses and eventually the inevitable happened. I shall never forget the first time we made love. I knew that I could never ever leave Jacob. We were soul mates bound together for eternity." Gino wiped away a tear.

After the telling of their sad tales, the two of them were not at a loss for things to talk about. The mood lightened, and the conversation continued with their likes and dislikes, and what kind of entertainment, books and music they preferred. In a very short time they knew all about one another.

As they were finishing their pasta course, Antonio said to Gino. "I have been so lonely since my partner died. Meeting you has been a Godsend."

Gino put his fork down and put his hand on Antonio's. "I feel the same way," he said.

Antonio smiled and said, "Let's not order dessert here. Come back to my place. I'll make coffee and I have some fresh pastry I bought this afternoon."

"That sounds nice, "Gino said.

When Antonio got the check, Gino tried to pay his half, but Antonio was insistent. "You can get it next time," he said.

Next time? Gino's heart was racing again at the thought that there would be a next time.

They walked slowly back to Antonio's apartment with Antonio holding Gino's arm. Antonio told Gino that he had moved here about two weeks before they met. The old apartment was too big and too expensive to handle alone. They didn't say anything more but they kept smiling at each other.

When they reached the front entrance of Antonio's building, Gino said, "This is very nice for me, being with you. I don't know how many more lonely evenings sitting at home I can bear."

"It's the same for me," Antonio said and there was a slight sob in his voice. "Will you be my friend? Will you go places with me and do things with me?" Gino ran his hand down Antonio's cheek and wiped away the tears.

When they were alone in the apartment, they stood facing each other awkwardly for a minute or two and somehow Gino got the courage to ask Antonio, "Will you hold me, please? Nobody has held me or put his arms around me for six years."

"Of course, Gino. I need you to hold me as much as you need to be held."

The two men embraced. At first they just held each other. They were both crying. Then they stared into each other's eyes and their lips met. In the beginning it was like a kiss you would give your baby sister, but little by little their passion took over. The kiss got stronger, more insistent, more passionate, and at last their tongues tasted each other.

"Will you lie naked with me, Antonio?" Gino pleaded.

"I want that too, so badly."

Antonio led Gino into his bedroom. All thoughts of coffee and dessert were put aside. They stripped and lay down in bed facing each other. They embraced and pushed their bodies close. Their semi erect cocks met and they ground them together. They ran their hands up and down each other's backs, especially caressing their buttocks. Their fingers reached down and found each other's cocks. Gently they started to stroke each other as they began to moan in old pleasures newly aroused.

" I want to suck your cock," Antonio said.

"Me too. Let's play sixty-nine," Gino countered. They assumed the position and took each other passionately into one another. They were each surprised at how hard they had become. As each one tongued the other, they played with the other one's asshole, stroking it and pushing a finger in occasionally. Neither expected it to happen, but they came almost simultaneously, swallowing every drop of the small amount of cum that each produced. They lay still for awhile, reluctant to give up the beautiful instruments they had in their mouths. Eventually they gave in to the inevitable. Antonio was facing the foot of the bed. He turned around to face Gino again. They embraced each other, and at the same time, in perfect unison, they said, "I love you!"

They lay holding each other, crushing their cocks together. They both produced more tears than they were able to produce of semen. Neither of them slept that night. They lay in Antonio's bed fondling and caressing one another all through the night, making plans for the future, just as if they were two young school boys who had a lifetime ahead of them.

In the morning Antonio made coffee with buttered rolls and jam. Then they showered together. Without care for the amount of water they used, they washed and explored each other's bodies until they were practically sterilized.

After they dressed they went to Gino's apartment for a fresh change of clothes for Gino. Instead of getting dressed, Gino got undressed and Antonio did also. They lay on Gino's bed, their naked bodies wrapped together, their arms caressing, their cocks crushed together, and their tongues in a fierce duel.

They didn't care in the least if they brought each other to a climax or not. Their only thought was to hold each other and experience the joy of having a loving male body to have and to hold again. Words cannot adequately describe their new found happiness. It was all the sweeter because each had gone from lonely despair to utter euphoria.

Shortly after noon, they reluctantly got out of bed and dressed. Instead of just a cappuccino or an espresso today, they decided to have lunch as well. They crossed the street and seated themselves at what used to be Gino's table. Antonio was more than happy to relinquish his old viewing spot.

They each ordered ante pasta and a cappuccino and settled down for their usual viewing activities, but instead they kept turning toward each other and smiling broadly, totally ignoring the eye candy on the street. Every so often they would giggle like children. Their silly behavior did not bother them at all.

After awhile, two handsome young men sat down at Antonio's old table. They each ordered a salad and an espresso. They kept staring at Gino and Antonio, smiling at them and whispering to each other. Finally one of the young men said to the older couple.

"Excuse me gentlemen. We don't mean to be disrespectful, but we would like to ask you something. We have just made the commitment to be life partners. Sitting here, observing your happy faces, we are inspired by the two of you. Can you tell us please how long have you been together?"

Gino and Antonio looked at each other and smiled. Antonio knew instinctively that if they told the truth, the young men would be disappointed so he spoke up quickly, before Gino could say anything.

"We have been together since the world began," he informed them. As if to emphasize that fact, he took Gino's hand and kissed it.

"Aah," one of the men said, "that is so beautiful." He leaned over and kissed his partner on the cheek. "You are a true inspiration," he said to the two older men. "Thank you."

"I wish you a lifetime of the same happiness we have shared," Antonio told them. "Love each other always." The two men smiled, thanked Antonio for his good wishes, and returned to their salads as Gino leaned over and kissed Antonio on the cheek.

After the men finished eating, they got up to leave. They smiled at Gino and Antonio, and wished them a good day. As soon as they were gone, Gino squeezed Antonio's hand, and said to him, "You are a sinful liar, but a true romantic. I almost told them the truth, which is something I now realize they didn't want to hear."

"You know," Antonio answered, "in true romantic style, I wish to tell you that I have had enough of butt watching. I'd much rather watch you. Let's go somewhere very private." They left the café, and arm in arm. They crossed the street and entered Gino's apartment.

"I want your cock for dessert," Antonio said.

"It's all yours," Gino murmured.

For as many days in the future as they could count, they made love in the afternoon. Butt watching hardly ever happened after that.

SNOWBOUND

Mildred and Arthur Stone had never been much for religious practice or church dogma. Nevertheless they were members of St. Matthew Episcopal Church. The church was just shy of five miles from their home in Minneapolis, but they rarely attended, not even Easter or Christmas mornings.

When Mildred was diagnosed with an inoperable brain tumor in their thirty-seventh year of marriage, Art was devastated. They had no family at all, except for one son in California. He lived in San Diego and they had not heard from him in almost ten years. When Tom first moved to the west coast, they stayed in touch and visited him once or twice a year. On one of their visits, Tom introduced them to his friend Carl Stanton. They immediately liked Carl, and Art even let Tom know that he had good taste in friends. Before the end of the visit, Tom told his parents that he and Carl had committed to each other and were planning on living together as soon as they could find a bigger apartment. Art was heartless thereafter. He called Tom a faggot and he screamed that Tom was a total disappointment as a son, and he and Mildred cut their visit short. This was something, he always regretted, but he didn't know how to reach out to his son to ask for forgiveness and reestablish any sort of relationship. He didn't even know for sure that Tom and Carl were still in San Diego. How was he going to inform Tom when Mildred's time came? Not, he guessed.

Mildred suffered terribly for nearly two years. Radiation and chemotherapy destroyed her frail body. At the end, she didn't know Art, or much else for that matter. Art was still working when she got sick, but he was eligible for retirement. He took early retirement and a reduced pension so that he could care for Mildred. He was five years short of social security when he retired, but he didn't mind. He took care of her like no one else could. If she drooled slightly when he fed her, he would immediately change the bed sheets and her night gown. No trained nurse could have attended to her needs any better. In the end she died on a chilly Halloween evening. She died in Art's arms as he sobbed hard and bitter tears.

Every fifth of the month, Art received his church bulletin which he usually tossed in the circular file. However, when he received the November issue he glanced through it. The funeral parlor had asked for his church affiliation and he thought correctly that there might be an obituary. There was a full page obituary for Father Alfred Cole's wife. She had died on the same day as Mildred. The obit went on and on about her contribution to the church community, and Art just scanned through it. At the bottom of the long article were two smaller obits. One was Mildred's which listed her year of birth, year of death, maiden name and the fact that she was survived by her husband of thirty-nine years, Arthur Stone, and a son Thomas in San Diego.

The other obit was even shorter. The deceased was Andrew Brown. He was sixty-two years old, died after a long illness, and was survived by his long time friend and companion, Russell Taylor. Art paid no attention to it. He never really read it, merely glancing over it.

An article on the back page of the bulletin caught his eye. Father Alfred, due to his own grief, was initiating a support bereavement group at the church beginning immediately after the New Year. The group would meet every Thursday at the church from 6 to 7 PM. After all the months of caring for Mildred, and without much else to occupy his time, Art decided to attend the first meeting.

He spent Thanksgiving and Christmas alone in his house, feeling sorry for himself. To his credit, he did think of trying to locate his son, but at the moment it was just too much effort for him. After many years of absence, he did attend Christmas morning services at the church, but slunk out of the church in an effort to avoid the pastor.

On the day of the first bereavement group meeting, he found a million reasons not to go, but his loneliness prevailed and he dragged himself to the church. He was the last to arrive. Besides the pastor, there were four others; himself, two other men and a woman. Father Cole passed a small 3 x 5 index card to each and asked that they write down their names, addresses, telephone numbers and E Mail addresses. Art was the only one without access to the internet.

Alfred began by introducing himself by his first name. He urged everyone to start with first names only so that the group would be more informal, and less stiffly organized. Everyone spoke for a short while, and told the group a little about themselves, and how long they had been widowed.

Alfred started. He had been married for forty-five years. He was seventy-one and not planning to retire until the church kicked him out. His wife was a wonderful person and he missed her terribly.

Janet Rogers neglected to give her age or how long she had been married. She didn't speak much about her husband and she didn't seem to be in terrible grief. Art concluded that she was here to get another husband quick. He figured that she was about fifty-five. Jake Farrell, one of the other two gentlemen was about sixty and Art thought that Jake was picking up Janet's vibes, and even if he was not interested in marriage, there was going to be some serious sex there if he wanted it.

After Jake spoke, Art had his turn. He had been married for thirty-nine years, and was sixty-two. He retired to care for his wife, whom he missed terribly. He had a long career as a mechanical engineer, and would have enjoyed his retirement if Millie hadn't died of brain cancer.

"I feel the same way," Russ, the last gentlemen, spoke up. "I'm sixty-two also and I could be enjoying my retirement as well, if I had a companion to share it with."

"Amen!" Art retorted. Those few words were the only cross conversation that had occurred up to that point. Then the group started to talk freely, just as if they were sitting in one of their living rooms. Each avoided getting too personal about their lost loves. It was enough that they felt and shared their grief without having to worry about any one of them saying the wrong thing. It was incredible how people never knew what to say to the bereaved, and invariably said the absolutely worst things.

Janet zeroed in on Jake, leaving Russ and Art to talk together. Alfred went back and forth between the two groups. When they first shook hands, Art had a warm feeling toward Russ. Russ had an engaging smile and warm brown eyes which were open and revealed a good soul. They spoke easily about their careers, and how much idle time they both had now. Both declared that their unions had been enduring and loving. There had been little room for outside acquaintances, something they both now regretted. As the hour drew to a close it became obvious that Russ was the more outspoken of the two and would take the lead when he wanted to find out more about Art.

"Have you eaten dinner yet?" Russ asked Art.

"No, I haven't," Art responded.

"Would you have dinner with me?" Russ asked in a very questioning way.

Art would have preferred to retreat to his self imposed exile, but he didn't want to be insulting, and he really liked Russ, so he agreed.

"There's a nice little restaurant right around the corner. The food is good and the prices are reasonable. OK with you?"

"Sounds like a plan," Art answered.

Whereas Russ was always outgoing, Art was very introverted. So that when, during dinner, Art realized how easily the conversation was going, he was amazed. They talked about nothing really; TV shows, movies, plays, musicals, their former work, etc. The time went so quickly, they didn't even realize that they were the last diners in the restaurant. As they split the check, Russ asked, "Would you like to have dinner together again before the next meeting?" And Art surprised himself by eagerly answering, "Yes!"

They exchanged telephone numbers and agreed to meet back at this restaurant at 6:30 Monday evening.

"I left my car on the church lot," Art said. "Where's yours?"

"Oh, I walked," Russ said. "My apartment is only one street away."

As the two men shook hands before parting, Art got the warmest feeling. Both of them displayed wide and happy smiles for the first time in many months. They both hated that the evening was ending.

On Sunday morning, Art decided to go to church. Subconsciously he was hoping to meet Russ there. It would be more accurate to say that he prayed Russ would be there. When he entered the church, he stood in the rear and scanned the people already there. He didn't see Russ, but remained in the rear, hoping Russ was still to arrive. He never did.

After the service, Father Alfred greeted him warmly and he was glad he had come after all. He even went to the social hour in the social hall. Several men and women came over to welcome him remarking that they had not seen him here before. Art actually felt good about being there.

That evening Art did something that was very atypical for him. He called Russ. When Russ answered he seemed genuinely happy to get Art's call. "I wanted to confirm our dinner date for tomorrow," Art white lied.

"Wouldn't miss it for the world," Russ beamed back right through the telephone wires.

"I missed you in church this morning," Art said in a gallant attempt to keep the conversation going.

"Gee!" Russ said. "I belong to St Matthew, but actually, I don't go to services there. I attend a different church, Metropolitan Community Church." Art had never heard of that church. "I read about the bereavement group through the St Matthew church bulletin, and decided to come by and see what it was all about." He paused and then continued. "Art. I am so glad I did. If I hadn't I wouldn't have met you."

That sent shivers through Art's body, in the most pleasant of ways. "Thanks for that," he said. "I feel the same way."

At dinner the next evening, they began to learn lots more about each other. Russ was one whole day older than Art. Both had attended Northwestern and had actually graduated in the same class. Art was a retired engineer. Russ was a retired high school physics teacher. Don't tell anyone, but they both loved opera. Each had let their subscriptions go when their partners got sick. They loved the music from the theater equally as well, also the philharmonic, art museums, and rock concerts. Neither one followed sports very much.

Russ asked, "If I can get a couple of tickets to the opera, would you like to go with me?"

"I'd love to go with you." Art answered.

When they said goodbye they gave each other a very chaste and manly hug as well as a hand shake. Every time Art shook Russ' hand a fire went through him. He couldn't understand it, but he liked the feeling.

The next evening shortly after dinner, Russ called Art. "Hey!" he said. "I got lucky. I've got two good tickets to Lucia for a week from Saturday night."

"Fantastic!" Art answered. "What do I owe you?"

"This one's on me," Russ answered. "You can get the next one." The next one? Art started to tear. In all his sixty-two years he had never before had a male friend to share anything with. He didn't know what to say so he said nothing. After a while Russ was prompted to ask, "Art, are you all right?"

"Oh yes, I'm just fine."

"Hey, are you doing anything special right now?" Russ asked.

"No."

"Have a drink with me?" Russ made it into a question.

"I'd be delighted."

"Great!"

Russ gave Art the address of a bar that was about half way between them, and they agreed to meet in half an hour. Russ was already at the bar when Art came in. They hung their coats on a rack in the vestibule and then embraced each other warmly. There was a small table in a corner and Russ led them to it. "There's no table service here," Russ said. "What would you like?"

"I'll get this round. It's the least I can do," Art said, and now discovered they both liked scotch and soda. As he walked to the bar, Art noticed that all the patrons were men. There were no women in the room. He also noticed that when he and Russ were walking to their table, Russ nodded at one or two of the men and they nodded back as if they knew each other, but in a very casual way. Although he was aware of this, he didn't think much about it. He was just happy to be with Russ.

Both men had driven here so they agreed to a one drink limit which they nursed until they couldn't anymore, and then Russ got them each a coke. Once again they were trying to prolong the time they spent together. They were both enjoying each other's company so much. It was characteristic for Russ to warm up to people he met casually, but for Art it was a new experience. He didn't want to question it. He just wanted to enjoy it. Eventually, they both figured it was time to go. Before they got up to leave, Russ put his hand on Art's. Ordinarily, if a guy had done that to Art, he probably would have flattened him, but he didn't even notice the 'indiscretion.' What Russ did was just natural. Wasn't it?

"There's a 'thirties' film festival at the Orpheum, and I think they're showing *Frankenstein*. Would you like to go tomorrow evening?" Russ asked Art without removing his hand from Art's.

"You're on, mister," Art answered. "That's my cup of tea."

"Good!" Russ said. "When I get home I'll check the show time and call you to make arrangements."

When he got into his house, Art hardly had time to remove his coat when his phone rang.

"Hey there," Russ's cheery voice echoed through Art's whole body. "The movie starts at 8:15. You're on the way from me to the movie house so what say I pick you up about 6 and we can have something to eat downtown before the show?"

Art wanted to say, "Come much earlier than that so we can talk and talk and talk." But how would that sound? So he just answered in the affirmative.

They ate a quick dinner at a Denny's right down the street from the movie theater. They both ordered a breakfast explaining that neither ever had a real breakfast at home. They laughed at learning they had yet something else in common.

Frankenstein had scared them both half to death, when they were kids. Now it was so corny that they giggled throughout the showing, as did most of the audience. Still, they had a marvelous time. They shared a big bucket of pop corn which Russ held on his lap. Every time one of them reached into the bucket for some popcorn, their hands would touch, but neither of them seemed to notice. After the show, even though the Minnesota night temperature was nearing zero, they found an open ice cream parlor, and ordered banana splits like a couple of kids. They took lots of time eating the splits, each wanting yet again to prolong the night.

This night Art laid his hand on Russ's hand as he said, "Thank you Russ for being my friend. I cherish every moment we're together."

"No need to thank me. I feel exactly the same way," Russ said as he put his other hand on top of Art's.

Russ drove up to Art's door and Art asked if he would like to come in for coffee. "I think not tonight," Russ answered.

"OK pal," Art said as he left the car, "I'll see you tomorrow at the meeting."

The next day was cold, windy, dank and generally miserable. Neither of the men cared to venture outside. They both spent the day lounging around, reading, and wishing the other one was there. Both played opera recordings on their stereos, and neither ever turned on a TV or a radio.

When Art arrived at the church, it was snowing lightly. He was surprised that his was the only car on the parking lot but he was much relieved to find Russ already there.

"I honestly didn't expect you guys tonight," Alfred said.

"Why not?" they asked in unison.

"Don't you guys listen to weather reports? There's a blizzard heading our way, and the authorities have asked everyone to stay indoors if possible." Of course, neither of them had heard the news.

"Well, as long as you're here we might as well have a meeting," Alfred said. It wasn't much of a meeting. They just sat around and chatted like three old friends. Alfred made a big pot of coffee and served it with some chocolate chip cookies. They were enjoying it so much that none of them realized that the one hour 'meeting' had stretched to a little over two hours. Finally they realized it was time to go.

Art and Russ bundled up. There was a door in the meeting room which led to the parking lot. When Alfred opened the door, they were all amazed. The blizzard was raging wildly. There was a complete white out. They couldn't even see Art's car. Alfred said to Art, "You're not driving out there tonight.

Would you guys want to stay in my house? It's just behind the church."

"No thanks," Russ said. "I'm right around the corner. Why don't you stay with me, Art?"

"I hate to put either of you out," Art said. Trying not to sound too eager he accepted Russ' invitation. He then reached into his pocket and gave Alfred his car key. Alfred looked at him questioningly. "That's in case I'm not around when the plows come. The men can move my car if they need to."

Alfred took the key and let the two men out. They had to hold on to each other to keep from falling. The snow blew into their faces like pellets of ice. The three minute walk took them almost fifteen minutes. Russ lived in a four plex apartment house on the first floor. When he let them into the vestibule, it took the strength of both of them to close the outside door. The noise must have disturbed Russ' across the hall neighbor who popped open her door. There stood an elderly lady who looked like a cherub.

"Oh Russ, darling," she said. "I was so worried. Thank God you're home."

Russ introduced Rosie O'Meara to Art and explained that Art couldn't get home because of the storm so he would be staying with him.

"Well, if you men need anything just knock," she said as she retreated into her apartment.

Russ' apartment had a living room, an eat in kitchen, a laundry room, one bathroom and a bedroom, but in spite of that it was quite large. Each room was way oversized. There was an air of lived in comfort here.

They stood in the hallway soaking wet. "Let's get out of these clothes," Russ advised, "before we catch our deaths. I'll throw everything in the dryer." Art stared at Russ as he took everything from his pockets and placed them on the hall table. He stripped naked in seconds, and didn't seem to be embarrassed about his nakedness at all. "What are you waiting for?" he asked Art, so Art emptied his pockets and began to strip also. Russ took all their wet clothes and tossed them into the laundry room. He ran into his bedroom, opened a drawer and retrieved two warm up suits. He tossed one at Art and started to don the other.

When they had been naked, they gave each other the once over like all men do when they see other men naked. They both observed the same thing. It was so amazing. They were both lean, muscular, six feet tall, brown hair, brown eyes. Both were circumcised and their cocks were about the same size at about five inches flaccid, although Russ suspected they were both slightly aroused because generally he was a little smaller. They knew that they were checking each other out and the moment was a little awkward so Art said for no reason at all, "I have a son, you know. He lives in California. I never circumcised him. I thought it was barbaric. He had the only uncut penis my wife ever saw." He laughed as he said that.

Russ laughed too. "Let's retire to the kitchen," he said in a very formal manner. "I'll make us some much needed hot chocolate." Art followed Russ into the kitchen and sat down on a chair. "Are you ready to tell me about your wife, yet, how you met, what your relationship was like and so on?" Russ asked Art. Art was so introverted that it shocked him that he actually wanted to tell this kind man about his life. As Russ set the table and prepared the hot chocolate, Art began his short narrative.

We met in my first class on my first day at Northwestern. I had an English class and when I walked in I saw her immediately. She was just beautiful. Her hair was naturally strawberry blonde, and her blue eyes looked like laser beams. I could tell she was tiny even though she was sitting down. Thank God I had come early. The desk next to hers was empty and I ran to claim it. We smiled at each other and introduced ourselves. After class, I walked her to the door and did the bravest thing I'd ever done in my life up until then. I asked her if she was having dinner in the school cafeteria that evening, and when she said yes, I asked her to have dinner with me. She accepted and the rest is history. We were engaged after the first semester. Neither of us had siblings and when our folks died we had nobody but each other. We lived a fairy tale life until Millie got sick. We had few friends and didn't need any. Millie was the first and only woman I have ever been with."

"What about your son?" Russ asked.

"That's a story for another time." Art evaded the question. As Russ poured the hot chocolate, Art asked, "How about you?'

"Well," Russ began, "I probably met Andrew a few hours before you met Millie."

"Stop!" Art rasped. "Did you say Andrew? Are you telling me that your lost love was a man?"

A look of great distress covered Russ' face. "How could you not know?" Russ asked. "I thought it was obvious. I even told you I attend a gay church."

"Oh, Russ, I am so sorry for my stupidity. I told you how naïve I am. When you used terms like 'my partner' or 'my companion' I thought it was because you had not formally married. I'm not a church goer and that didn't bother me in the least.

"Are you bothered now?" Russ looked at Art pleadingly. Art took Russ's hands in his and answered, "Not in the least, my very dear friend. If you were a lion and I was a kitten, I'd still cherish your friendship. It's just that things are so much clearer to me now. Please, please, continue your story."

"I found my dorm room and I entered without knocking. I just didn't think that my future room mate was there already. I creamed my pants at the sight of him. All he was wearing was a pair of boxer shorts. He was about 5'10" tall and built like the proverbial brick shithouse. He faced away from me while unpacking a suitcase, which was lying on his bed and his bubble butt just bounced all over the place."

As he spoke about Andrew, Russ kept squirming in his chair adjusting his sweat pants. It was obvious to Art that Russ was sporting a good size erection, and he smiled at the thought. He wondered why he hadn't gotten erect thinking back to Millie.

Russ continued. "I quickly closed the door behind me to preserve a little of my room mate's modesty. He stuck out his hand and we introduced ourselves. He told me to make myself at home and stripped off his boxers. As soon as he did, I got a hardon that wasn't going to quit without my relieving it. I asked him why he did that and he told me that he hated clothes. He never wore clothes in private and he loved the feel of his cock slapping against his inner thigh when he walked around in the buff. Most important, he said that he wanted to see my reaction when I saw his giant cock, and he was overjoyed to see the tent in my jeans. Just like that he told me he was gay and would prefer to have a gay room mate. He went on to say that he had had some childhood experiences with his little friends, but he had never had real sex with a mature man. He intended to remedy all that in college.

"I told him that I was gay too, or at least I knew that to be a fact. I had up to then never had sex with any male, child or man, and I hoped to remedy that in college also. We laughed like hyenas. I knew we were already in love. That very first night we fulfilled our fantasies. It was all we could do to tear ourselves apart and go to classes the next morning. I swear, Art, neither of us ever slept with another guy from that day on."

When Russ stopped talking, Art started to blubber. His shoulders heaved in gigantic sobs, and he had trouble catching his breath. Russ ran to him and embraced him so that Art's head was resting on his chest.

"What's wrong, Baby?" Russ wanted to know. Baby???

"I did a terrible thing and I've regretted it for ten years, but I can't rectify it."

Russ ran his hand up and down Art's back and Art was comforted by the sensation. "Tell me what you did baby? Let me help you."

Art had stopped sobbing and could talk a little. Slowly he looked up at Russ, and in a faltering voice he said. "When my son, Tom, told me that he was gay, I thought he chose to be that way because Carl, his partner, had lured him into that life style. Oh Russ, I turned my back on him. I threw him out of my life when he probably needed me the most. And now in a twist of fate, worthy of an O'Henry story, I find myself hopelessly in love with a gay man. I tell you this in utter confusion, not even knowing if it's possible for me to perform a homosexual act or to even believe that two men can be in love. I always believed that gay men were in it simply for the sex. Until now I never believed that two men could actually love one another."

"You love me?" Russ gasped and pulled Art tighter to him. "I love you too and I thought I could never love again. Do you believe in fate my darling man? It's almost like Millie and Andy went away so we could be together for the rest of our lives." Art started to cry again and Russ continued. "I want to make you a pledge, my love. I promise you I'll never ask you to do anything that disgusts you, or grosses you out, or that you simply don't want me to do. I only want to be with you and to be your companion in whatever way you allow me."

Russ raised Art's face to be even with his. "I have an uncontrollable urge to kiss you," he said, "if you'll let me." In answer, Art stood up and faced Russ. The two men embraced and pressed their bodies together so that each could feel the other's erections. When they did so they ground themselves together as Art hungrily gave his first kiss to another man. They kissed gently at first and then their lips parted as their tongues caressed.

Russ led Art to his bedroom. When they got inside, he removed his sweat suit and helped Art remove his. They gently stroked each other's cocks as Russ lay Art gently on the bed. Art could not believe how good Russ's cock felt in his hand. "Let me do all the work," Russ said. "Just follow my lead. Did you ever have oral sex with Millie?" Art shook his head. He was too excited, or was he too scared, to talk?

"That's what I thought," Russ said. "Lie on your back." He was standing at the side of the bed leaning over Art. His tongue started to explore all of Art's body from his lips, down to his toes. When he nibbled on Art's nipples, Art began to squeal like a piglet. He tongued all around Art's cock, his balls, and his inner thighs but never touched Art's throbbing rod. When he finished sucking on Art's toes, he told Art to roll over. Then his tongue explored all up and down Art's back. He kissed Art's cheeks over and over, each time coming closer to Art's crack. Eventually, he parted Art's cheeks and his tongue began to slide up and down his sweet opening. Art was going crazy. He began to dry hump the bed and it was all he could do to keep from cumming. Instinctively Russ knew that he wouldn't ask Art to reciprocate in any way until he wanted to, so he turned Art on his back again, leaned over him and took his tool as far down his throat as he could. Art's moans could be heard above the roaring wind beating against the window. As he slowly pulled his mouth up and let Art's cock slip out of his mouth, he ran his tongue up and down the shaft. He kissed the head and sucked Art's flowing precum out of him. When he pushed back in all the way to the base he stopped and pumped the base of the shaft gently with his lips. All the while he held his fingers to Art's lips and Art instinctively knew he was supposed to lick them. When they were moist, Russ found Art's crack with his middle finger and gently massaged it. When he felt it relax a bit, he gently inserted it a little. Art's body tensed but he didn't push Russ' finger away. Suddenly Russ' finger slipped in a little and then as if Art's ass became a vacuum, it sucked Russ' finger all the way in. The sensations Art was feeling were beyond his wildest dreams. Russ sensed he was going to cum and stopped sucking. Instead he cupped Art's balls and started licking and sucking them. Art's body was convulsing and writhing in sheer ecstasy. He started to scream, "I need to cum. I need to cum." Russ took Art's pulsating cock back in his mouth and sucked as sensuously as he could. He felt Art's balls withdraw into his scrotum as he let out one wailing scream and came and came and came in Russ's mouth. Russ swallowed as much as he could, but saved some for Art. He leaned over Art's face to kiss him, and let Art's cum drop into his waiting mouth. Their tongues lapped up the remaining cum as they both basked in this ultimate moment of intimacy.

They lay side by side fondling each other's cocks and balls. Russ was almost afraid to ask, but Art was so silent he had to know. "Are you happy darling?" he asked Art. Art turned to Russ. "I've never been happier."

"Do you think you would ever want to do that to me?" he asked fearing the answer.

"Yes, that and lots more. You'd better be a good teacher so I can give you as much pleasure as you just gave me."

"Teaching you is going to be so much fun. You know, it would be just fine with me, if this snowstorm never ended." They both fell into a deep and peaceful sleep for the first time in years.

Art woke up the next morning wondering where he was. When he regained his senses he smiled in deep contentment. He was alone in bed so he jumped out to look for Russ. He didn't have to look far. Russ was standing in the bedroom doorway totally naked. He was grinning broadly at Art and he sported a good size morning woodie. He was holding a piece of paper in his hand. He ran over to Art and embraced him in a bone crushing bear hug. They kissed, totally ignoring morning breath. Then he showed Art the piece of paper. "Here's Tom's address and telephone number," he said. "He lives in Los Angeles with a Carl Stanton."

"My God!" Art Gasped. "How???"

"I Googled him," Russ proudly announced. Art did not have a clue what he was talking about so Russ brought Art a little bit more into the twenty-first century.

"I'm going to have to break down and get one of those new fangled things," Art quipped, but Russ said seriously, "No need; you can use mine." More hugs and kisses.

"I'd suggest you wait until tomorrow to call him. It's Friday and he's apt to be at work." Art nodded in agreement. "By the way, the snow hasn't let up at all. I checked the weather report and it's not expected to stop until the wee hours of tomorrow morning." Art glanced out the window. It was still a total white out.

"I guess we're stuck with each other," Art said. Russ led Art into the bathroom. He gave him a new toothbrush and they brushed side by side, bumping their hips together playfully.

"Wanna shower with me?" Russ asked with a leer.

"Uh huh."

Russ adjusted the temperature in his stall shower and they stepped inside. Each one soaped the other. Art followed Russ's lead and inserted his soapy fingers into places that would have appalled and disgusted him yesterday. But today he was eager to accept and give the pleasure it generated. Then he shocked Russ. He fell to his knees and took Russ's very hard tool into his mouth. He sucked on it as Russ had sucked on him the previous evening. Last night the lovers had fallen asleep with only Art having been satisfied. Russ had planned it that way so now he was so horny, he couldn't control himself. He began to pump Art's face wildly even though he knew he should be gentler. Art loved the taste of Russ' prick. He couldn't believe the sensations running through his body, and when Russ shot his load instants later into his mouth, he gulped down as much of the sweet juice as he could and then stood up and shared the rest with Russ. They kissed wildly, each yelling, "I love you" to the other, and both crying tears of joy.

"Please fuck me," Russ begged Art. For one split second, Art experienced a moment of reticence. Then he looked at Russ' soft brown eyes and knew it was something he wanted to do. He nodded at Russ, who smiled and turned toward the shower wall. He put his hands on the wall and bent his still firm ass toward Art. He told Art to stretch him by inserting a soapy finger into his love canal. That was easily done, and Art was instructed to insert another. That was no problem either. "I guess I'm still stretched after all this time," Russ said in wonderment. "Now soap up your cock and place it at my opening." Art happily obliged. Russ reached around and encircled Art's cock with his hand and guided it slowly in. There was a little resistance at first, but once the head was in, the rest glided right down to where Russ could feel Art's pubes. It tickled and he started to giggle.

"What's wrong?" Art sounded concerned.

"Nothing, but we are going to have to trim our pubes," Russ answered still laughing. "Now," he said, "Just pump in and out just as if you were fucking a woman," Russ instructed. Art barely heard him. He was off somewhere in another world. Millie had never been this tight, especially after Tom was born. She would try to tighten around him but he could barely feel the friction. As a result they didn't have sex too often since neither really enjoyed it that much. Art found more pleasure in a hand job. Some sixth sense caused Russ to keep contracting his love abyss especially when Art's cock rubbed against his prostate. To his great joy and surprise, Russ found himself about to shoot a second time. At his age it was an unexpected pleasure. He shot a good size load against the shower wall. As he did so he contracted even more around Art's cock and Art came with one long scream of pleasure. He stayed inside of Russ as long as he could but nature finally forced him out. He whispered in Russ's ear, "When will you do that to me?" Russ was completely spent. All he could say was, "Soon, babe, soon."

They spent the day eating what canned food Russ could find in the house, listening to music, and frolicking in bed. Eventually Russ initiated Art into the joys of anal sex. Art wouldn't admit how much it hurt at first, but Russ had told him to expect this so he said nothing. Eventually he relaxed and began to enjoy the sensation. When his prostate was touched he went wild. "No wonder gay guys love this so much," he whispered, and Russ was pleased. Before they even decided to retire for the day, whatever fears, reticence or prejudices Art had previously had about male sex, they were all shattered. He loved how he felt, but especially he loved Russ, and the feeling was mutual. At one point they wondered how they would explain this to Father Alfred and why they were dropping out of the group. They decided to tell him the whole and honest truth.

The next morning the snow had indeed stopped, but it was still windy and overcast. There was no sunlight to shine on the newly fallen snow. The streets were still unplowed and the wind blew the snow into formidable drifts. It was obviously going to be another snowbound day. The new lovers couldn't care one iota.

Art waited until 11 AM to call Tom. It would then be 9 AM in LA. He fumbled so badly punching in the numbers that he had to start over several times. Finally, Russ took the phone and said, "Let me get him on the phone and speak to him for a minute, I'll pave the way and then you two can talk."

The phone rang in Los Angeles and after the third ring, a strong male voice said, "Good morning, whoever you are." Russ had to smile.

"Good morning to you. Is this Tom or Carl? ......Carl, I'm glad it's you. My name is Russell Taylor. I'm a very dear and close friend of Tom's dad." He said it in such a way that he hoped that Carl, being gay, would get his innuendo. He continued, "Tom's dad, Arthur, would like very much to speak to Tom and tell him how much of a fool he's been and ask for forgiveness. Could you kind of pave the way for them as I'm trying to do?"

There was silence on the phone for a moment and then Carl let out a scream that even Art could hear. "Russell," he said. "We ran out of orange juice and Tom just went out to get a few things at the super market. Please give me your number and I'll have him call right back. You have no idea what this is going to mean to him. We have a wonderful life together, but he's always lamenting the fact that his parents can't see how happy he is, how happy we are." He made Russ repeat the number three times to make sure he got it right.

Art sat by the phone ringing his hands. "What if he doesn't call?" he worried.

"He'll call. You heard what Carl said. He's been dreaming of this moment for a long time." He pulled a chair up to Art's and held him tightly. About ten minutes later the phone rang. Art fumbled with the hand set but managed to get it to his ear.

"Hello," he croaked so that he could hardly be heard. But he started to sob and those sobs could be heard loud and clear at the other end.

"Dad, dad, please don't cry. Talk to me. I need so much to hear your voice," Tom urged.

"Tommy, Tommy, boy. I am so sorry. Can you forgive an old fool? I've regretted every minute since I lashed out at you and I was too stubborn to call you back." He kept repeating, "Please forgive me."

"Of course, I forgive you. I could never hate you. I just want to see you and mom so bad. Please come out here for a visit soon."

"Tommy, boy. I hate to tell you this but mom passed away almost three months ago. I didn't know how to reach you, but my friend, Russ, Googled you in seconds. I swear son, I didn't even know what that meant. I need you to forgive me for not letting you know."

Tom was crying softly and Art could hear Carl saying, "Don't cry, baby, I'm here for you." Art wanted to stick a knife in his heart. How could he ever have dared to try to deny Tom's love for this caring soul?

He heard Tom say, "Dad I forgive you for everything. I love you to death. Just knowing that you're all right with me and Carl and our lifestyle, well, that mean's the world to me."

"And me," he heard Carl yell in the background. "I want you to come for a visit, please. I'll pay for everything. Just come."

"I can't wait, Art said, "but I can pay my own way. Can I bring my friend Russ? Without him, I never would have found you."

"Absolutely, Dad. We've got a guest room and a day bed in the den so there's plenty of room for all of us."

Art took a deep breath. His moment of truth was about to occur. He looked at Russ proudly and smiled at him. Then he said to Tom, "Tom, about sleeping arrangements," He hesitated for a second. "One bedroom will be fine for Russ and me."

There was utter silence on the other end, and Art began to tremble until he heard Tom roaring with laughter. "Why you dirty, horny old man," he laughed and laughed. Then seriously he asked. "Are you happy, Dad?"

"Yes, very much so. I think Russ makes me as happy as Carl makes you."

"Then you have our blessing. Could I speak to Russ for a minute, Dad? We want to thank him for what he's done."

Art handed Russ the phone. "Tom and Carl want to speak to you."

"Hi," Russ said, a little nervous for the first time… "There's no need to thank me… Yes, we'll be out as soon as we can… Call anytime……We love you too… Do you want to speak to your dad again?"

He handed the phone to Art. "Yes, I'll call again soon… We'll let you know when we are coming as soon as we book the flight… Yes we'll do it today… We love you too, son. Goodbye for now."

Art fell sobbing into Russ's waiting arms. "God sent you to me. I'll never doubt him again. I'm so happy on so many different levels, my heart is going to explode," he joyfully announced to Russ.

"I'm just as happy as you are, baby. I always wanted a son. I'm going to spoil him silly," Russ joked.

They laughed until they cried. When they both calmed down, they spent hour after hour demonstrating how much they loved each other. Even though they could have left sooner, they spent two more days in the apartment.

A ROAD TO NOWHERE

How often had the man heard the expression, *A Road to Nowhere?* It had never really sunk in. After all, it was nothing more than a poetic expression. Roads can't go 'nowhere.' They usually have a beginning, a middle section and an end, wherever that end may be. *Just like the yellow brick road*, he thought.

So where was he going? He was thoroughly lost. But isn't that what he wanted all along? To be alone. Wasn't that the entire reason for this trip? In spite of the fact that there was no light at the end of the road, so to speak, he had no choice, but to trudge right along. He could not go back, and he was reluctant to get off the road. He had to believe that every road had some destination at the end, after all.

In a short while he came across a fallen tree that had been pushed to the side of the road. *That would make an excellent bench to rest on*, the man thought. He removed his knapsack and laid it down near the tree. Then he sat down and his thoughts wandered back to a month earlier, and to the events which brought him here.

James Bannerman was an account executive at one of Madison Avenue's largest and most successful advertising agencies. The pressure on him was enormous. Long hours and constant deadlines had taken a toll on him. His wife of only one year had walked out on him. The first night, or I should say the first early morning, he returned to an empty home, he suddenly started to hyper ventilate. He could not breathe. Lucky for him, he was able to call 911 before he passed out.

Even luckier, the heart attack was very mild and little damage was done. It was a strong warning to him to stop abusing his body. He was discharged in a mere four days with strict orders to take several weeks off and get plenty of rest, relaxation and recreation. The agency wasn't happy but they gave him an eight week sabbatical.

His sister was a travel agent and the two of them poured over travel brochures, and a myriad of escorted tours. He rejected them out of hand. He definitely wanted to be alone and away from people. He did, however, examine the pictures carefully, and he fell in love with Scotland, or at least, the look of Scotland as pictured by the travel industry. With a little bit more research, Arlene booked a bed and breakfast for him, miles from the nearest large city. After arriving in Edinburgh, he would have to rent an auto and travel almost forty-five miles to the inn. That was exactly what he wanted.

The inn was everything he dreamed it would be. It was small, quaint and remote. It was surrounded by English gardens and was picture book pretty. There were only two other guests, a honeymoon couple from London. He barely saw them, even at breakfast.

He spent his days sitting on the veranda with a blanket wrapped around his legs and a good book in hand. He was happy and content for about three days, then boredom set in, and he decided to take a hike. Right after breakfast the inn keeper packed him a picnic lunch and he started up one of the several paths that led away from the inn.

The early autumn air was crisp and a bit blustery. He loved it. It felt so invigorating. He walked for about two hours. Taking deep breaths of the refreshing air, he didn't notice that the path had ended and he was walking in a small clearing surrounded by groves of trees. For a second he panicked. He had paid no attention to the direction he was walking in, so even if he could use the position of the sun to establish the direction of his return route, he didn't know what that direction was.

He tried to remember if the sun had been in front of him or to the rear, to the right or to the left when he started out, but no memory was afforded him. All he could do was to turn around completely and start walking in a reverse direction. He walked for hours, through clearings and through groves, but he never found the path he had been on. Finally, as twilight was upon him, he stumbled on a paved road, just wide enough for one auto going in one direction.

If I follow the road, he thought, eventually I will come to some civilization. Suddenly he started to laugh. Maybe he'd be lucky enough to find Brigadoon and marry Cyd Charisse. The thought warmed and amused him, but he had to make a decision in which direction to start walking. For no reason at all, except for a hunch, he turned right and renewed his trek until he came upon the tree trunk.

He decided that he had rested on the tree trunk long enough. His food was long gone and it was time to move on. He put his knapsack back on and continued on his confused way.

According to his watch, it was ten o'clock at night when he saw something up ahead. He was certain he saw a light, but then it seemed to disappear. He hurried his step, and there it was again. It was definitely a light, but this time it was brighter and did not disappear. As he got closer, he could see that the light came from a small cottage. *Thank God*, he thought. I'll be able to call the inn from there to come and get me.

As he drew nearer and nearer to the cottage, it became prettier and prettier. Surely kind souls dwelt there. He sprinted the last one hundred yards to the front door. *Thank goodness the lights are still on*, he thought. A beautifully carved knocker adorned the front door and he began to knock.

The door was answered by a tall, very lean, very distinguished looking gentleman in his late thirties. Bannerman thought that he was probably five to seven years older than he was.

The man smiled at James. "Don't tell me you're lost," he said. "If you are, you'll be the second lost tourist this week. He broke out into a hearty laugh. "Come in, come in," he said waving Bannerman in.

"Take off that knapsack and get comfortable," the man said. He extended his hand. "I'm Ian MacBeigh," he said. "Are you hungry? I've got plenty to eat and drink."

"I'm starved," James said, "but mostly I am so damned thirsty."

"Would you like plain water or a little wine?" Ian asked.

"Water please," James responded. Ian went to a small refrigerator and removed a pitcher of water. He poured a generous amount for James, and the two men sat down at a small table. Everything in the cottage was small.

"I can give you a ham sandwich with cheese if that will do." Ian told James.

"Oh my, yes. That will do just fine."

"Are you staying at the Olde Wayside Inn?" Ian asked.

Bannerman nodded. His mouth was full.

"I'm afraid I have no phone. The road back is partly paved, partly dirt and partly grass fields. It's too dangerous to negotiate in the dark. I can drive you back in the morning and I can only offer you my hospitality and shelter for the night."

"That's more than kind of you," James said gratefully.

"Have you ever slept with a man before?" Ian asked.

James looked aghast. "Wh… what?" he asked.

Ian broke out laughing. "I meant that in the literal sense. I only have one bed, but it's big enough for both of us." James relaxed and joined Ian in laughter.

"It's not too late," Ian said. "I'm starved for company out here. Would you join me in a little conversation over a mug of beer before we turn in?"

"I'd be delighted," James said.

After the beers were poured, the two men sat on two easy chairs in the front room. "You look like a very urbane American," Ian said to James. "What in the world brings you to our remote part of the world?"

For some reason James found Ian easy to talk to and he found himself relating the whole story. He told him how his wife had walked out on him, about his mild heart attack and how he had chosen this region for the sheer beauty of the pictures he had seen. "Now you look too young to be retired so what brings you here?" James asked Ian.

"I was afraid you would ask," Ian said jokingly. "I teach English Literature at the University of Edinburgh. About six months ago my world was turned upside down and I had a nervous breakdown. I was forced to take a year's sabbatical. This cottage was my weekend getaway, but for now it's my home for another few months."

"I wouldn't mind spending a few months here. It's the closest thing I've ever seen to Paradise," James said.

"That would be wonderful if you could," Ian said. "At one time I had someone to share this edenic spot with, but now I'm alone." Ian grew quiet, and James allowed him his moment of reflection.

"If you don't mind my asking," James said. "What was it turned your world around?"

"It's funny," Ian said, "until now I had not wished to speak of it, but you are so easy to talk to and I feel like getting it off my chest, so here goes."

Ian poured some more beer in each of their glasses and began: "First of all, James, I can tell you this because you can't run away, and you're stuck here for the night. I'm gay." He stopped to see James's reaction, and looked at James inquiringly.

"Relax, friend," James said. "I'm in advertising. I interact daily with gay male models, gay photographers, and gay copy editors and so on. I figured you were gay the minute I got here. For a straight guy, I have excellent gaydar."

Ian did indeed relax and he continued. "I met Fergie (Evan Ferguson) in college. I was majoring in English Lit and he was into mathematics. We began studying together, and it didn't take long for us to discover that besides both of us being gay, we had fallen hopelessly in love with each other. I know you here about promiscuity in the gay community, but Fergie and I knew each other for nearly a year before we made love. He was my first and my only. I will never forget that first night with him as long as I live.

"We were both very lucky in procuring teaching positions at the University. We bought a house together and were as happy as the proverbial pigs in shit. We both had the jobs we wanted, the lover we wanted, and the house we wanted. We had it all, but Jamie my boy, don't ever get too complacent. One day, returning from work, Fergie was hit broadside by a very drunk teen ager. He was killed instantly. I was a useless bag of shit after that, and the University ordered a year off for me."

Ian buried his head in his hands and broke out sobbing. James was never a touchy, feely person and he wasn't even consciously aware of what he did next, but he got up, went over to Ian and put his arms around him. Ian put his arms around James and sobbed on his shoulder.

James took Ian's beer glass and his own and washed them in the sink. When he returned to the living room, Ian was still crying. He stood him up and said, "Let's get you to bed."

When they entered the bedroom, James began to laugh.

"What?" Ian asked.

"Am I the first guy you have slept with since Fergie?" He said it with a smile, hoping to lighten the mood and perhaps get a smile out of Ian. It worked. Ian looked at him and said with a wide grin, "In the literal sense, yes."

They both stripped to their boxer shorts and Ian pointed the way to the bathroom. James went first and then Ian. When Ian got back to the bedroom, he found James standing there.

"Why aren't you in bed yet? I promise. You are safe if you want to be."

James had the good grace to laugh. "I was just waiting to see which side of the bed you wanted."

"How kind of you," Ian said. "I always slept on Fergie's right side," he said.

"Then so be it," James said. He crept into bed and Ian followed. As he got into bed, Ian turned off his bedside light and the room was in darkness. Although their bodies never touched, James was in a state of utter nervousness. Ian fell asleep immediately, but it took James quite awhile.

James had no idea what time it was when something woke him. As soon as he got his bearings, he realized that Ian had rolled over and thrown his arm around his chest. In so doing he had nested against James, who literally froze. He thought that maybe Ian was dreaming, and thinking that he was Fergie. He wanted to give Ian that pleasant dream so he didn't push him away. Besides, there was no harm done if another man held him. In fact, it was kind of comforting. He and his wife made love and then turned away from each other. They had never held each other like this and James kind of liked it. He liked it, that is, until he felt Ian's erection against his thigh.

Once again he panicked, but soon relaxed. Nothing was going on and nothing was going to. The problem was that his own manhood was as stiff as a steel rod.

Ian went on sleeping soundly, so that after awhile James relaxed enough to fall asleep also. Ian's arm was still thrown around James.

Ian awoke first. He was surprised and a little upset to find his arm over James's chest. James was still sleeping and Ian didn't want to disturb him so he decided not to move. Lying still, he dozed off again. He dreamed that he was nesting against Fergie. His hand wandered down to find Fergie's very hard cock. He began to caress it playfully.

In his sleep, Jamie began to moan. Someone was doing wonderful things to his cock. He felt an orgasm coming on. It was going to be a good one, he could tell. He not only felt it in his groin, he felt it all over his body. His wife was smothering his body and playing with his cock like she never had before. At last she was making love to him, not just having sex.

He came all over Ian's hand, his underwear, his own thighs and the bed linens. The two men woke with a start. Jamie was still euphoric from his orgasm, but Ian realized immediately what had happened.

"Shit, shit, shit," he yelled. "I am so sorry." He jumped out of bed to get a towel, but James grabbed his hand.

"Easy man, relax. I needed that badly and it was great. There's no need to apologize and don't panic. I loved it." He let go of Ian who ran to get the towel. When things were somewhat dried up and cleaned, James found himself without underwear, lying naked in bed. He motioned for Ian to join him. Ian removed his boxers and got into bed with James.

"That was fun," James said. "Let's play some more. Jamie liked it."

The two men faced each other. Their bodies rubbed against each other. Ian's erect cock was grinding into James's groin, and James's flaccid cock was getting hard again.

"This is incredible," James sighed. "I never knew." Ian leaned over and kissed James. At first James wanted to recoil, but he didn't and moments later his tongue was playing dueling swords with Ian's. He was shocked to learn that he was enjoying kissing a man.

When Ian felt that James was hard again, he leaned over him. Ian's tongue began to explore James's neck, then his nipples, then his navel and finally his inner thighs. James was moaning and tossing his body around. Ian wrapped his tongue around James's cock head and then down his shaft. James had gotten a few blow jobs in college from girls, but never anything like this. Much to his very temporary dismay, Ian removed his mouth from James's cock and began to suck up and down his crack, occasionally inserting his tongue into the hole. James was moaning and screaming and Ian knew what to do. He took as much of James's seven inches into his mouth as he could. He ran his tongue up and down James's shaft, and it didn't take long before James had another pulsating orgasm. This time Ian swallowed all of it.

The two men lay back exhausted. "You taste so good," Ian said to James. "I have missed Fergie so. Do you think that you would ever want to do any of that stuff to me?"

"It can be arranged. I'm certain," James answered and leaned over to kiss Ian. He tried to repeat everything Ian had done to him, but he hesitated before each new maneuver. He thought it would be disgusting and that he would think it was gross, but a whole new world was opening up to him. He couldn't believe how good Ian's cock tasted or his cum or his ass hole crack. James was walking on air, or at least floating on the bed.

"When I was eleven or twelve, my buddy and I began to explore our sexuality," James explained to Ian. "We tried inserting our tiny penises into each other's asses and even occasionally licked our cock heads. Eventually my friend had an orgasm in my ass and then I did the same. After that we fucked as often as we could. It was fantastic sex, but neither of us thought we were gay. At about fourteen, we just stopped doing it, and I simply put it out of my mind, and went on with my *straight* life. You have helped me rediscover an aspect of my life I had buried, and like I said before, "Jamie likes it."

"I'm pleased," Ian said, and the two men went right on exploring each other's bodies and their sexuality."

Eventually they showered and dressed. After breakfast Ian drove James to the inn, where he packed up and moved out. Of course, he moved in with Ian.

The next day, they drove to Edinburgh for food and other supplies. Ian took James to see his city apartment. There he showed him pictures of Fergie. "God he was so good looking. What do you see in me?" James asked.

Ian laughed. "Crazy man," he said. "You're much better looking."

When they left the apartment, Ian took James for a walk around the neighborhood. While the two men idled away the time window shopping, Ian asked James, "Since advertising is so stressful, if you could do something else, what would you do?"

James looked up and down the busy little street they were on. "I think I'd like to own one of these little shops along this street," he said. I'd get to know everyone in the neighborhood and get home at a decent time to a restful place with a loving mate. My God, look!" James pointed to a sign in the window of a small tobacco shop. The sign read, "For Sale."

There was a sweet smell of tobacco emanating from the shop. In the window the shopkeeper had dozens of beautifully carved pipes for sale. The shop was more of an antique pipe shop than a tobacco shop. They went inside. The owner had exotic pipe tobaccos from all over the world. James was getting heady from the aromas.

"This place is fantastic," he said to Ian. I want to buy it and live with you forever. If I go back to what I was doing, I'll be dead in a short time. Besides, I don't ever want to be too far from you. I love you."

Ian ran out of the store. James ran after him. He worried that he had moved too fast and Ian would hate him. Ian was sobbing. James put his arm around him. "I'm sorry," he said. "I'm too impulsive."

"Shut up, you crazy man. Buy the damned store, if you can afford it, but don't apologize for loving me. I love you too."

James had his sister, Arlene, ship him all his clothes and a few personal things from his Manhattan apartment. He paid his landlord to break his lease, and asked him to donate his furniture to charity. He became a resident of Edinburgh. He never lost his New York accent and the residents referred to him as that crazy American. Ian even got him a job at the University teaching Foreign Advertising three hours a week. After awhile he found himself teaching advertising on a full time basis. He had to hire a young lad to run the shop for him.

No life is ever stress free, but James came damn near close to it. As far as he was concerned, he had visited Scotland, traveled a road to nowhere, and found his Brigadoon. Furthermore he now preferred Ian MacBeigh to Cyd Charisse.

MOONRISE

I love the twilight hours, when the moon starts to rise in the heavens. For me it is the most romantic part of the day. For most of us, it marks the end of the work day. It is time to kick off your shoes and lie back, and show that special someone just how much he means to you.

I had left my office late that Friday afternoon, gearing up for a romantic evening with my partner Troy. In fact, I was gearing up for a romantic weekend. We had both agreed to turn down all invitations and spend the entire weekend at home, making love. We arranged to meet at our favorite gay bar for TGIF drinks before holing up for the weekend. Our Friday night dinner was in the refrigerator and all it needed was heating up. "All I need is heating up," I thought with a smile.

I arrived before Troy, and had to fight my way to the bar, because the place was so crowded. Several friends grabbed me along the way and insisted on some sort of conversation. It took so long to get to the bar that I figured that even if Troy came late, he was probably here by now. Optimistically I ordered a drink for me and one for him. With drinks in hand, I started to fight my way from the bar. I looked for a couple of free inches to stand and wait for him. The few tiny tables in the place were all occupied.

I found a spot near the front door where I could place the drinks on a small ledge, built just for that purpose. I also had a partial view of the entrance so I could keep an eye out for my guy. I was a little worried because it was kind of late for him.

I was sipping my gin and tonic when I heard the noise. There was a screeching of brakes, followed by a very loud thud. Instinctively I knew that it wasn't two cars colliding. I had never heard a sound like that before, because I had never before heard a human body being hit by a moving car.

Loud as the noise was in the bar, I distinctly heard screams from the pedestrians on the street. I put my drink down on the ledge next to Troy's and pushed my way to the front door. I had a terrible feeling in my gut.

I could see the form of an adult male lying on the road and another man standing over him and sobbing. "I didn't mean to do it," the man cried. "He ran right out in front of me. There was no way I could stop and I was going so slowly. Oh God. Oh God."

The form in the street was covered with blood, but there was something familiar about the tattered tweed jacket he was wearing. The dread in my stomach was taking over the rest of me. I began to panic and ran toward the dead man. Strong arms grabbed me and restrained me. I tried to break free but they were too strong for me. Finally I conceded defeat and stood with the army of rubberneckers in abject silence. It took about ten minutes for the ambulance to get there and I stood stunned, completely in a state of shock.

The EMT's put the body on a stretcher and covered it with a plastic. "Does anyone know the victim?" one of them asked. I stepped out of the crowd sobbing. They tried to question me, but soon realized that I needed medical attention myself. They put me in the ambulance and I sat next to the body. One of the technicians sat next to me and tried to ask me questions, but I couldn't process what he was asking me, and I was useless.

Finally he asked me what the victim's name was. "Troy Farraday," I sobbed out.

"I've got his wallet right here," the EMT said. He looked in and said, "I'm afraid it's a match." My sobbing grew stronger.

"Are you related to the deceased?" he asked.

"I'm his partner," I said barely above a whisper.

"Who is his next of kin?"

"I am."

"I mean does he have any blood relatives?"

"Troy was raised in foster care. He never spoke of any blood relatives. I am his only family."

"Look, the EMT said. I'm going to list you as his first cousin. When we wheel him to the morgue, just follow me to make the identification. Let's keep it our little secret. I've seen enough of these domestic partnership situations to know how unfair they are. I don't mean just gay couples, but unmarried heterosexual couples too."

"Thank you," I said. "I am truly grateful." I resumed chest heaving sobs and the EMT put his arm around me.

We reached the hospital and I followed the EMT to the morgue. The man in charge filled out a bunch of papers and it seemed like hours until he was done. They put Troy on a gurney and eventually he would be put into a vault until the funeral home claimed the body.

The kind EMT removed the plastic from Troy's face and I nearly fainted. He was so covered with blood and his face was so disfigured that I could not make a positive ID. I asked the EMT if I could see Troy's fingers. He exposed both hands and the corpse was wearing the matching wedding band we had given each other after we had committed to one another. We had gone to a nearby church, kneeled down before the altar, read wedding vows to one another, and exchanged rings. Maybe government didn't recognize our union, but we did, and so did God.

All the while the EMT was standing by me. If I could have thought clearly, I would have wondered why he wasn't off again saving a life or two. The pathologist instructed me to make funeral arrangements ASAP and to arrange with the morticians to pick up the body. I was in a trance. I just nodded and started to leave when I fainted. When I awoke, it was I who lay on a gurney. Standing at my side, holding my hand was the EMT. He looked in my eyes and said to me. Hi Buddy. My name is Warren. How are you feeling?

"I'm OK," I croaked.

"You're all right to leave, but I don't think you should be left alone." He leaned down and whispered in my ear. "Look," he continued. "My car is at the fire station. I just need to return the ambulance and I'll drive you home, so you come with us." I was too weak to object and I knew I needed help getting home. I needed to face the task of arranging the funeral and that would take all my strength.

"Thanks," I said. "You are so kind. Why are you being so good to me?"

"I'm gay too. My partner was killed in Iraq and I know what you are going through. It's the very least I can do."

As we left the hospital, and Warren and his fellow EMT were helping me into the ambulance, another ambulance drove up to the emergency entrance. The EMT's wheeled another bloody man out of the ambulance. At least this one was alive, but not looking too good.

Troy Farraday was just putting on his jacket, preparing to leave his office to meet his partner, Luke, for TGIF libations. Just then a west coast client called to get some much needed information. He realized the time difference and was apologetic, but he assured Troy that he would only be a minute. The minute became more than half an hour. After he hung up, Troy ran out of the building. He knew a short cut to the bar. If he ran through the alley way between his building and the one next door he didn't have to go all the way up First Avenue and cross at 31st Street to get to Second Avenue. He would already be at Second, and the bar would be just a few yards away.

He sprinted through the alley. None of the late afternoon sun filtered through either of the two buildings. It wasn't black as night, but it was darker than twilight in the alley. Troy did not know what hit him. He was struck from the rear with a crowbar. His assailant hit him over and over again until he lost consciousness. The assailant then stripped off Troy's tweed jacket, his gold wedding band and, of course, he took his wallet.

While the perpetrator was beating him, some of Troy's blood sprayed on his forehead. He was not aware of it. When he had taken what he wanted he ran toward Second Avenue. Before he reached the street, he saw a clear opening in the traffic which would enable him to make it across the avenue without stopping at the curb. Just as he reached the curb, the blood on his forehead dripped into his eye. For just a moment he was blinded and so he failed to see the car that had just pulled away from the curb. He was hit. His body flew up in the air and landed several feet forward, moving with the car. By the time the driver could stop the car, he had run over the crook another time.

It was almost a half hour before someone else used the alley as a short cut and discovered Troy's bloody, comatose body. He called 911. Another half hour passed before the EMT's arrived and sped toward NYU Medical Center.

The ambulance carrying Troy arrived just as Warren was helping me into his ambulance. When we arrived at the fire station, Warren had to hand in some reports. He sat my robot like body on a comfortable chair. Finally, when he was ready to leave, he helped me to his car and started out.

"Where do you live?" Warren asked, realizing that he had taken his report so mechanically that he didn't remember where the victim had lived. I told him where my apartment was and Warren commented that he lived a few streets away, and that I was actually on his way home. Warren was lucky enough to find a parking spot in the crowded street, and helped me up to my apartment.

"I'll make some tea," Warren said.

"I'll make it," I said, and I put water up to boil in a tea kettle. I also set the table. I placed a tea bag in each cup and sat down to wait for the water to boil. Suddenly my chest began to heave and I started crying again. Warren stood up and took me in his arms to comfort me. I cried more softly and finally said to

Warren, "I have dinner for two in the fridge. It just needs to be heated. Would you like to stay for dinner?"

"Yes, I would. I don't want to leave you alone. Come let me help you."

Preparing dinner helped me get a hold of myself. The two of us busied ourselves setting the table and heating the meal of pot roast, roasted potatoes and creamed corn. I took some rye bread out of the freezer, and put it in the microwave to defrost.

I began to talk about Troy. I told Warren how we met, how we fell in love, how much we loved each other. My eyes were teary as I spoke but I didn't cry again. Then Warren started to talk about his dead partner, Matt. Their love affair was equally torrid, but Matt was in the army. Matt had a two week furlough and went to New York where the two men met in a gay bar. After Matt was discharged, he relocated to New York and they moved in together. Unfortunately Matt was a reservist. His unit was reactivated and deployed to Iraq, where he was killed by a land mine less than two months ago.

We both began to cry and we held each other tightly.

"Troy was so fastidious about everything. I can't believe he would be so foolish as to step out in front of traffic like that," I said.

"Maybe he was so anxious to get to you, he dropped some of his guard. We'll never know, will we?"

After dinner we cleaned up and sat down on the sofa. Neither of us talked much, but I kept sobbing. Warren held me tight. Finally he said, "I don't want to leave you alone tonight. I'm off for the weekend. How about I camp out on the sofa?"

"Would you? I'd like that. I can give you a new toothbrush and some underwear and stuff that would fit you," I said. "But the sofa is uncomfortable. I have a king size bed so there's plenty of room for the two of us," I told Warren. "You can sleep in the bed."

"OK," Warren said. He looked at his watch and said, "Holy mackerel. It's past midnight. Let's turn in."

We went to the bathroom together. I have a double sink and we brushed our teeth standing side by side. We spoke a little. I can't remember what was said, and Warren called me Matt and I called him Troy. We actually laughed at our Freudian slips.

I asked if he wanted to shower and he said he was too tired and suggested we shower in the morning. When we got to the bedroom, Warren stripped completely. I was surprised and I guess he noticed. "Oh, I'm sorry," he said. "I always sleep in the nude and I just didn't think." He reached down to get his shorts, but I said, "No don't bother. I always sleep nude too."

We both climbed into bed, but neither of us slept. I was sobbing as silently as I could, and I distinctly heard Warren do the same. Without realizing what we were doing, we turned toward each other and held one another tightly to comfort each other. Even if our cocks touched, we were unaware of it. We were both flaccid and sex was the last things on our tortured minds. We fell asleep holding each other in a comforting embrace.

At the hospital, they could find nothing on Troy to identify him. They labeled him John Doe and began a battery of tests. They were relieved to diagnose severe contusions on his skull, but there was no internal bleeding and as far as they could tell, there was no brain damage. They wouldn't be sure of anything until he awoke from the coma. They couldn't even be sure if he would ever awaken from the coma. They hoped that some family member would inquire after him and identify him. He was an obvious crime victim and the police wanted to interview him as soon as they could.

Warren and I tossed and turned fitfully. We slept a little bit, but the sleep was far from restful.

At about 2 AM Warren asked, "Are you asleep, Luke?"

"No," I answered. "How are you feeling?"

"Sad, blue, you name it. Luke, I find that when I can't sleep if I whack off, it helps me relax and fall asleep. If you think you would like to do it, I can go in the other room."

"You need it as much as I do," I said and my voice cracked. "Let's do it together." As I suggested that we masturbate together, I pushed the covers down with my feet. "Troy, my love, I miss you so much," I cried out loud. I started to whack off, but I was crying so hard, my stroking was useless. Warren was doing the same with equally unsuccessful results.

"Here," he said. "Let me help." He reached over and started to play with my cock and balls. He stroked a bit and tickled a bit and I actually got aroused. When I was partially erect he began to stroke and I hardened even more. I reached over and took his flaccid cock in my hand and did the same to him. Soon he too was hard. We stroked for awhile and I was getting close. It must have been pure reflex because without any conscience intent, I leaned over and took his cock into my mouth. As I did that, Warren twisted around into a sixty-nine position and devoured me. It wasn't long before we both came and we drank every drop of the other's cum. Warren turned around and we lay side by side.

I pulled the covers up and leaned over and kissed Warren. "Thank you, Warren," I said.

"Thank you," he answered and we both fell into a peaceful sleep. Warren's sleeping solution had worked for us both.

Troy remained in a coma all night. Early in the morning, he was bathed by a male nurse who was not afraid to really clean him. He changed his linens and gave him a fresh hospital gown. When he was satisfied that the coma patient was comfortable, the nurse left the room.

Troy opened his eyes. He had no idea where he was, but he knew he was in a bed, a hospital bed. "I'm going to be late meeting Luke," he thought. Then he fell asleep. It was not the sleep of a coma, but an ordinary sleep. His body was so traumatized and exhausted that he slept until late morning.

Warren and I did not wake up until about the same time as Troy.

"Are you upset about what we did last night?" Warren asked.

"No, no," I assured him. "We needed to comfort each other, and we did. I don't believe either one of us is ready to start thinking about a new relationship. That doesn't mean we can't be friends. Come let's take a shower and I'll make breakfast. Then please help me make funeral arrangements. I don't think I can handle it alone." We showered separately.

When Troy awoke, he immediately called for anyone to help him. Two nurses rushed in smiling.

"I need to pee," he announced. The male nurse helped him out of bed and to the bathroom. When he was put back in bed, he barked. "What do you have to do to get something to eat around here?" Then he started to cry.

"How did I get here? Why does my head hurt so much?"

"You were beaten up and apparently robbed. The police will want to question you," the nurse informed him.

"I'm afraid I won't be much help. I don't remember anything and I sure didn't see who or what hit me," Troy explained. "Oh God, did anyone inform my partner?"

"I'm afraid not. We don't even know who you are. You had no ID on you," the nurse said. "How about enlightening us while we wait for the neurologist."

The nurse took out a pad and proceeded to get as much information as Troy could give him: name, address, social security number, Health Insurance Company, etc.

Warren and I were making arrangements at a local mortuary when Troy called home. He got the answering machine and left a message. Then he called my cell phone, but I had turned it off so as not to be disturbed during the preparations for Troy's funeral.

When the arrangements were done, Warren volunteered to take me to lunch and I gladly accepted. As we left the funeral home, I turned on my cell phone. "One missed Call," the screen informed me. I retrieved the message. I listened and I thought that this was someone's idea of a sick joke. I listened again. It didn't sound like a joke. I asked Warren to listen.

He turned white. "Holy shit," he gasped. "We better get to the hospital and quickly." On the way to the hospital, Warren pulled out his cell phone and called the police. Then he called the mortuary and put a hold on the funeral arrangements until an unexpected development could be verified.

Warren took us in through the emergency entrance where everybody knew him. We rushed up to Troy's room. His head was bandaged, his eyes were black and his chin was blue, but it was Troy, for sure. I wanted to grab him, but he looked so fragile that I was afraid. Gingerly I embraced him and he hugged me back, but I heard him groan. Obviously he was in pain. Warren just stood by smiling at us.

When at last we could talk, I introduced Troy to Warren. I told Troy all that Warren had done for me when I thought he was dead and I couldn't function on my own. I omitted to tell him that we had sex together.

Troy held his hand out to Warren and thanked him profusely for having cared for me. In a short while two police detectives entered the room and flashed their badges. They were wise enough not to interrogate Troy or ask too many questions. They just let him talk until he told them all he knew. While Troy was talking, I didn't see Warren slip away. When he returned he had a plastic bag containing Troy's wallet and gold ring. "I retrieved it from the morgue," he said. "They have changed the corpse's name to John Doe pending an ID. The police are going to finger print the body."

Just as the police were leaving, the doctor arrived. "Hi," he said brightly to all of us in the room. "I'm Dr. Ryan. I need to ask you a few questions. First of all, what's your name?"

"Troy Farraday." The doctor looked at me and I nodded.

The doctor then proceeded to ask a slew of meaningless questions like where Troy lived, where he worked, who was the Governor of New York, who was the President of the United States, etc.

"Good," the neurologist said. "I don't believe there has been any brain damage. We'll keep you here for a day or two for observation and then you should be good to go." He left abruptly.

I turned to Warren. "I'm staying with Troy. I'll sleep on the chair, but you should go home and get some rest."

"OK!" Warren said, but I'll be back first thing in the morning. He gave me a big hug and said, "I'm so happy for you, for both of you, I really am." Immediately, my brain, which was composed of romance cells, began to search my memory banks for a suitable someone to fix Warren up with.

I didn't know where the time had gone to, but the commissary staff was delivering dinner to the patients. Unfortunately, Troy was stuck with a liquid diet. I wasn't very hungry but I went downstairs to the cafeteria and got myself a sandwich and a coke. I gobbled down the food so I could get back to Troy. I sat down in the chair at his bedside, and held his hand. We looked out the window to see the moon rising.

"Beautiful sight," I commented.

"I agree," Troy said and he tightened his grip on my hand.

I began to cry. "I thought I had lost you." I lay my head down on Troy's chest and he ran his finger through my hair. I could feel that he had put his ring back on. I sat up and kissed him full on the lips. Holding his hand, we both stared out the window watching the moon rise. "I love you," I said.

"I love you more," he replied.

SEDUCTION

Look! Let's get something straight (excuse that word). Just because I'm gay, single, thirty-two years old, and have never had a serious relationship in my life, does not mean that I don't want the American Dream for myself. I'm a successful attorney and I believe I deserve it all, just like any straight, married couple. I want the house in the country, the rooms to furnish and decorate, the flower beds to putter in, the lawns to mow, and the horrific morning commute to negotiate on my way to work every day. Simply stated, I want it all.

Why not? I told you that I'm a successful attorney. I work for one of the most prestigious firms in the southeast. I expect to be made a partner before I am thirty-five. Trust me, that's a major accomplishment. So why shouldn't I want it all?

I was renting a small apartment, which was just a short walking distance from my office, when I suddenly, very badly wanted to own a place of mine. I started looking at downtown condos, but the condo commando restrictions were amazing and I really got turned off. I started perusing the real estate ads for private homes. My friend Mac must have taken me to see a thousand re-sales. Mac is a fuck buddy and a real estate agent. He is just like me, relationship challenged. Anyway, I couldn't find anything that I really felt I wanted to live in.

As a last resort, I started to look at ads for new construction. One Sunday morning, I saw an ad for a development in the suburbs, but within easy commuting distance to my office. If the ad was accurate, the home prices were compatible with my budget, and they had no less than eight models to select from. I finished my breakfast quickly and jumped in the shower. As it was part of my morning routine, I whacked off in the shower. Just because I was going house hunting didn't mean that I had to deviate from my habits.

The first thing I noticed when I entered 'The Haven' was the absolutely beautiful entrance. I think they must have imported every flowering bush and tree from tropical Africa. Once I managed to get through the man made forest, fountains and waterfalls, there were certainly enough signs directing prospective buyers to the sales office.

At the moment, I was the only prospective buyer in the office. Two eager sales people jumped up to greet me. One was a very handsome guy in his early forties. I wanted him to be my salesperson, but the woman beat him out. She was also very attractive, about twenty-eight or nine years old.

"Hi, I'm Nancy," she said extending her hand. I shook her hand, but for some ornery reason I didn't feel like giving her my name. I guess I was mad at her for denying me the pleasure of the handsome salesman. Nancy was not about to be defeated. She handed me a card to fill out. It requested the usual vital information, name, address and telephone number. Nancy won round one.

"Can you give me an idea, what you are looking for by way of housing? It would help me a great deal."

"I'm looking for a one story house, not too big, but on a big lot. I'm single and don't need a lot of space."

Nancy's face clouded over and I knew just what she was thinking. I told you. I'm a lawyer. I can read people's faces. Nancy was thinking, just like all of you, that single people are not serious buyers. She would have added an exclamation point to that if she knew I was gay.

I smiled sweetly at her and in my most sincere lawyer voice I said, "Nancy, let me assure you, I am a serious buyer." Nancy looked shocked. After all, I had just read her mind.

Let me cut to the chase. I ended up buying a ranch style three bedroom home, with a Florida room. It was on a cul-de-sac so my lot was pie shaped. The front yard was not large, but the back was huge. I could even add a swimming pool to the back yard if I was so inclined. As an added attraction, the builder was able to save two huge shade trees at the back of my property, which gave me a little extra privacy.

Once he had my down payment, the builder seemed disinclined to rush completion of my house. But if you learn to be patient, you can get by. One day, almost nine months later, I took I ride out to 'The Haven' to check the status of my investment. Voila! The cul-de-sac would have five houses on it when completed, and all five were under construction. The cul de sac would consist of three colonials and two ranches. Six months after that date, I was the first of the five to move in to my new home.

It took me a few weeks just to unpack my boxes. The job was so overwhelming, that I just couldn't get going on it, so I set a goal of two boxes a day. Miraculously the number of boxes lying around began to diminish. The garbage service had advised me that they would not take corrugated boxes unless they were flattened. I flattened today's allotment of boxes and was schlepping them out to the curb for pick up, when a car drove up to the house on my right and parked along the side walk. It was followed by a huge moving truck. Whoever these people were, they would be the second of the five cul-de-sac residents.

The wife was the first out of the car. She was about twenty-four or five years old. She was a dead ringer for the way Debbie Reynolds looked in 'Singin' in the Rain.' So you have an idea how cute and perky she was. The husband must have been occupied with something in the car because it took him a couple of minutes to get out of it. When he stepped out, I knew that I was in for big trouble. I could never live next door to someone so beautiful and so sexy and maintain my sanity. Let me describe him, although words are truly inadequate.

He stood six feet tall. He was wearing cut off shorts and a tank top shirt. The ripples on his chest rivaled the number of waves in the ocean. His biceps were huge and bulged out indecently. His thighs and calves were so muscular that unless you looked twice, you would think he had piano legs, but then you realized it was all muscle. His brown hair was cut short in a buzz. Even from a distance, I could feel his sexy brown eyes giving me the once over. His nose was chiseled, his chin square, and he had a day's growth of beard. Ah, do you think that I did not check out his package? The shorts were old and worn, and the contour of his crotch was so evident that I had to will my erection away. Fuck, fuck, fuck! Why did he have to be straight.

When I was able to come down to earth, I saw that they were approaching me with the obvious intent of introducing themselves. I got myself together and started walking toward them. The woman spoke first.

"Hi," she said extending her hand. "My name is Marla DeAngelis, and my husband's name is Nicholas."

"Nick!," he corrected her curtly.

"Hi guys, my name is Eddie Gilbert. It's a pleasure to meet you." I shook Marla's hand and then reached for Nick's. His grip was so strong, I thought he would break all the bones in my hand. He seemed oblivious to his strength.

"Wow," I said, "Are you a physical fitness instructor?"

"Yeah. How did you know? You must be psychic or something. I own my own gym on Ash Street. Marla here, is an executive secretary for a big manufacturing company. What do you do?"

I heard the question, but my mind was so busy getting a membership in Nick's gym that I hesitated uncomfortably too long. Finally, back on earth, I said, "I'm a lawyer. Promise not to hate me." They both had the good grace to laugh.

"Where's your wife?" Nick asked, looking all around.

"Sorry," I said, "there is no Mrs. Gilbert. I'm single, but looking." Why did I say that? Marla would be sure to have me for dinner with every one of her single girlfriends. Dummy, dummy, dummy!

To change the subject, I asked, "While the guys are moving you in, would y'all like to come in and I'll make us something cold to drink?"

"Oh no thanks," Marla said. "I've got to show them where everything goes, but why don't you two guys get acquainted. Take Eddie up on his offer, Nick."

Nick seemed relieved of some terrible burden, and gladly accepted my invitation provided that the cold drink could be a beer. I assured him that his wish was granted and we went into the house, where I knew I would not be able to keep my hands off him. Please God, help a poor horny soul.

We sat at the kitchen table and I opened two bottles of Bud Light. Nick took one long swig, belched unceremoniously, and declared, "That sure tastes good on such a hot day. You gotta feel sorry for those poor sons of bitches hauling all my furniture."

He pushed his chair away from the table and sat on it with his legs stretched out. His short shorts were ever so revealing. The bastard wasn't wearing any underwear and I could see one of his balls peeking out. I am positive, in fact I'll bet you whatever, that he did that on purpose, because he was checking me checking him out. Do you know how hard I had to fight to keep from grabbing his crotch? I tell you, I was in agony. The worst thing is I believe he knew it, and he was showing me no mercy. My forehead was drenched in sweat, and my own shorts were bulging.

He certainly sensed my discomfort, because he put a look of concern on his face and asked me, "Is something wrong? You don't look so good."

I wasn't going to let him play with me like that so I simply said, "I'm fine."

Then he got bolder. He took a sip of the beer, holding the bottle with his left hand. As he swigged at the bottle head, he did two very suggestive things. First he laid his right hand on his enormous bulge, and second, after he took a swig, he began to lick the bottle head with his tongue like he was licking a cock head.

How thick could I have been? It would have been obvious to any casual observer that Nick was trying to seduce me. It should have been the other way around, but I was fighting the urge to do so. Still I couldn't be certain that I was right, and if I made a move on this colossus, it might be the last move I would ever make. Then he got even bolder.

"I know you're not totally settled in yet," he said. "I can tell from all those unopened boxes, but I sure would like to see the rest of your house, if you don't mind." That would mean standing up and exposing my erection to him. At this point I didn't give a shit. Besides, I was sure he was in a similar state.

"Sure," I said. I led him through the dining room, living room, Florida room, and the two extra bedrooms. I had set one up as a true bedroom and the other I had made into a home office. I even showed him the guest bathroom. He was merciless.

"And where does the big kahuna sleep?" He asked.

My bedroom door was closed. I hadn't even made the bed that morning, but he gave me no choice. I opened the door and let him in. The first thing I saw was a tube of lubricant on the bedside table. I had used it when I whacked off that morning. I had been watching male porn on the TV. The TV set faced my bed and I had happily whacked off while watching two young studs fucking and sucking.

Apparently Nick saw the tube also. He walked over, picked it up and asked me, "Is this what you use when you jack off?"

I'd be damned if I would answer such a personal question so I remained silent.

"Don't be shy," he said, "I use lube myself, when I jack off. I shouldn't be telling you this, but Marla really doesn't know how to satisfy a man so I take matters into my own hand." He laughed uproariously at his little joke. I was not amused.

Then, as if he had not tortured me enough, he turned toward the master bath. "I need to pee," he said. "Beer does that to me." Without another word he marched into the bathroom. He did not close the door, but turned away from me so that his rear end faced me. He dropped his shorts and aimed whatever he had at the toilet bowl.

That ass was beautiful, superb, two orbs of heavenly nectar. I wanted to grab them in my hands and squeeze them. I wanted desperately to kiss them and run my tongue up and down his crack. I didn't dare. I just tried unsuccessfully to look away. When he was through peeing, he shook his thing vigorously. I still couldn't see it. What size? What girth? I couldn't tell.

Then, he did something I would never have expected. He crumpled a wad of toilet paper and thoroughly cleaned his ass hole. It was like an invitation to put my tongue in as far as it would go. The man was driving me crazy and I had no idea if he was even aware of what he was doing. At last, he brought up his shorts, washed his hands, and asked if he could have another beer.

We went back to the kitchen. Again he sat on a chair which he pushed away from the table. He spread his legs, resting one hand on his crotch again. The conversation lulled. Finally he said that he should go home and see if he was needed. He got up with his half finished beer and started to leave.

"If they don't need me, is it OK if I come back and we shoot the breeze some more?" he asked. I wanted to scream, no, no, no! But I just nodded my head meekly as he left. I collapsed on a chair and tried to catch my breath. As soon as I felt that my legs would indeed support me again, I got up to go to the bathroom to jack off. I was badly in need of relief. But before I could do that, there was a knock on the kitchen door. It was Nick.

"Marla practically kicked me out and told me not to come back for at least three more hours," he informed me.

"Come on in. It's nice to have company," I lied. "Want a fresh beer?" He nodded and smiled broadly at me. He resumed his earlier position and started on his beer.

"I've been thinking," he said. "You've got a pretty nice physique, but you're lacking in the muscle department. Why don't you join my gym and I promise to buff you up. I'll give you a great big discount. If you want, I'll be your personal trainer. There's a benefit comes with that. I personally do your massages."

I was about to cream my pants, but I nodded, and in a mere whisper I said, "That sounds like a plan!"

"Good," he said. Then we both started talking about our plans for our houses, and suddenly his legs were not spread and he didn't seem to be teasing me anymore. Thank you, God.

"I'm planning on putting in a swimming pool as soon as possible," he informed me. "Swimming is a great exercise. I have a pool at my gym," He continued. "I think I'll surround the back yard pool with very tall, very thick bushes so Marla and I can skinny dip."

I pictured that scene, and grew weak again. I began to relax some and to enjoy Nick's company. Somehow the time went quickly and he went home to pay the movers, and help Marla get the place in living condition.

At long last I was alone. I went into the bathroom and very slowly and leisurely started to whack off, all the while imagining that Nick and I were playing a hot game of sixty-nine. I am sure that his cock was much bigger in my imagination than in real life. Ah heavenly bliss.

After that I saw very little of Marla and Nick. We were all busy with our jobs and setting up our households. I did go over to their house once or twice to help Nick put up some shelves and he returned the favor. Marla, gratefully, never did try to fix me up with a girlfriend. At this point I had a suspicion that Nick might have guessed that I was gay.

A few weeks after they moved in a crew showed up next door with back hoes and bulldozers. Nick had gotten his permits and construction on his skinny dipping swimming pool was getting underway. Almost at the same moment, a moving truck pulled up on the other side of me. My other next door neighbors were moving in.

They were a couple in their thirties, Jane and Marvin Carrington. They had twin girls, Casey and Kelly, aged ten, a good looking young boy, Shawn, aged seven, and a mutt named Scamp, aged two. Well, don't feel sorry for me. I said that I wanted it all, and if the American dream includes screaming neighbor's kids and barking dogs, well so be it.

I really was still so very hot for Nick that I decided to take him up on his offer to join the gym. I found out that the gym was open from 5:30 AM (to get the before work crowd) until 10 PM (to get the after work crowd.) Needless to say, Nick's hours were erratic. It would take some juggling of my time if he was to be my personal trainer. I called him at work and arranged to come in that very day after work to sign up and set up a training schedule with him.

Nick was true to his word and a true friend. He charged me 50% of the going rate for my membership. We scheduled for me to come in every Monday, Wednesday and Thursday evening after work. The sessions had no set time limit. I told him I would begin my training the following Monday if that was OK with him.

On the following Monday evening, I arrived at 5:30 and went to the men's locker room. I had been assigned a locker so I changed into a sweat suit with only a jock strap underneath. I placed my clothes neatly in the locker and went out to the gym to find Nick.

Nick was spotting a young teen ager who was pumping iron. As he stood over the young man it was obvious that the teen was trying to see Nick's package because he was gawking at it. I had already established that Nick did not wear underwear. I wondered if he wore a jock strap in the gym.

He was just finishing up with the boy. When he approached me he enveloped me in a bear hug. I swear, he made sure I could feel his cock press against me. He started me easy. He gave me ten minutes on an exercise bike and ten minutes on a slightly inclined treadmill. Both were set at a moderate speed. Then he took me over to the weights. He attached a five pound ring on each side of a bar and had me lie down under the bar. Following his instructions, I gripped the bar and raised it until my arms were straight. Nick was standing directly over me. I wanted to cry. He was wearing a jock strap. I raised the bar and lowered it so many times I lost count. When it was raised, Nick stood ready to catch it should I suddenly let go. After some time I begged for mercy.

"You did good for the first time," he congratulated me, as he slapped me lightly on my back. Oh that slap felt so good. Who cared if his grammar sucked.

"Now," he said, "we don't want those muscles cramping up so let's give you a short massage. *'Make it a long one,'* I prayed.

Nick led me to a back room which served as the massage room. He told me to strip and lie face down on the table. I stripped to my jock strap, and he laughed. "Do you want a good massage or one that forces me to avoid vital areas? Ditch the shyness and take off the jock." I was helpless. I did whatever he said. I could not remember when I was more self conscious. Nick seemed to ignore my nakedness. I guess he was more than used to naked clients.

Whatever you or I were expecting, forget about it. Nick gave me an ordinary, straight (hah) massage. Then he told me to go to the locker room, shower and dress.

"If I don't see you in the neighborhood first, I'll see you here Wednesday evening," he said as he bid goodbye to me. I drove home, wanting to cry all the way.

For two weeks our sessions went just as I described except that my exercises got longer and harder and the weights got heavier. Then just as I was ready to give up because I was getting nowhere with Nick, I got a pleasant surprise.

As he was massaging me one Monday evening, Nick said, " The pool is finished and ready for use. Marla and I were going to initiate it tonight, but she had to accompany her boss on a business trip. How about you and me breaking it in tonight?"

All I could think of was that I didn't want to spend another hour with this man in utter frustration. I had long ago fallen in love with him, and being so near to him was sheer torture. However, all my mind allowed me to do was to picture skinny dipping with him. I could not say no to him and nodded my head.

"What time?" I asked.

"Well, I'm leaving right after you do. What do you say we have dinner together? I'll throw a couple of steaks on the barbeque. You can bring the beer and pretzels. How does that sound?"

"It sounds good. I say yes," I answered him with a big grin and a very bold slap on his rump. I did that without thinking, and regretted it immediately. I was pleasantly surprised when he ignored the love tap and said, "I'm looking forward to a guy's night out with you. Come on over as soon as you want to."

I nearly crashed my car twice on the way home. My head was spinning. I knew that it would be a chaste evening, but I had reached a place of resignation. If I couldn't have Nick physically, I would settle for close proximity.

I came over wearing only my swim trunks and was pleased to see that Nick wore only a skimpy pair of gym shorts. Did he have on a jock strap? I didn't know for sure. He had started the steaks, and was garnishing them with garlic powder and steak sauce. He was also barbequing corn on the cob. I was carrying a case of cold beer and I had laid two bags of pretzels on top of the beer.

I helped Nick lay out plates, utensils and napkins on his picnic table. When everything was ready, he put the steaks on one platter and the corn on another and brought them to the table. I had already opened two bottles of beer. The table sat four people, two on each side. I sat down on one side in the middle. Imagine my shock when Nick pushed me over and sat on the same side of the table as I did. I was surprised and happy, but I cringed. He was back to teasing me, and I liked it, I hated it, I was sure of what he was doing, I wasn't sure of what he was doing, I wanted to kiss him, I wanted to cry.

Somehow we got through dinner. I can't tell you how many times his leg brushed mine or his arm bumped into mine. I lost count, but I was getting hotter and hotter and ever so unhappy. We cleaned up our mess, and went back to the pool. We each sat in a lounge chair letting our food digest, just as we had been taught to do as children. Nick made small talk, told me how pleased he was with my progress and reached over and felt my bicep by way of confirmation.

Without any warning, he jumped out of the lounge and took off his gym shorts. He had a throbbing, raging hard on. He was about eight inches, and so hard he was pointing at his belly. Although most of his cock head was out of the sheath, I could tell he was uncut. His cock definitely matched the rest of him. He grabbed me and pulled me out of my lounge. Before I could react, he had pulled down my swim suit and I stepped out of it. Of course, I was as hard as he was, and I heard him gasp. He had seen me flaccid, but never erect. You see, I never told you, but I have ten uncut hard inches and it's wider around than most men I have seen or have ever been with. Mac, my fuck buddy, has trouble taking it up his ass, even after all this time.

When Nick was finished staring, he jumped in the pool and beckoned for me to follow. I am afraid I had enough of his teasing. I loved Nick but I was getting very resentful of what he was doing to me. I had definitely reached my breaking point. I was determined to confront Nick no matter what the consequences were. I just couldn't go on living this way. I told Nick to please come out of the pool. We needed to talk.

"Why so serious?" he asked.

We both sat down on the lounges again, facing each other. Nick was dripping wet. Just looking at the beads of water running down his rippled chest was turning me to mush. It took all my courage to start talking first.

"Nick," I said, "you know I'm gay, don't you?"

"Yes, of course."

"Then you must know how you have been torturing me."

"Yes."

"Then why the fuck are you doing this to me?"

Nick thought for a while as if trying to find the right words. Finally, he began.

"After I signed the contract to purchase this house, Marla went to the room where they kept the samples. They asked her to select tile, cabinets, paint colors etc. I was alone with Nancy and asked her if any other houses on the cul-de-sac were sold yet. She told me about you and said she was certain you were gay. I said to myself that I wasn't going to live next door to no faggot. I ran to get Marla to break the contract. I was ashamed to tell her why. We had twenty days to legally void the contract. Marla wouldn't hear of it so I was stuck with the house.

"When we drove up on moving day, I saw you standing there. Marla jumped right out of the car to meet you, but I hesitated. I didn't even want to shake your hand for fear you might infect me. Then I got an idea. I decided that I would flirt with you and get you all hot and bothered, but for sure, all you were going to get was blue balls. That first day in your house, I was having a picnic. I could see how uncomfortable I was making you and it was all I could do to keep from laughing.

"Later on, when we began to help each other with odd jobs around the house, I kinda forgot you were gay. I began, little by little, to see you as my next door neighbor and eventually, a friend. I don't know why I kept torturing you. It had become a habit with me, I guess, and I just couldn't seem to stop.

"One night, I was making love, correction, having sex with Marla, and I began to fantasize having sex, correction, making love to you. I wasn't upset or appalled or anything. I really wished that it was you. I didn't know how to act on it. I had never had any desires for a guy before and I was afraid that if you didn't feel the same way, you would laugh at me. I can stand rejection but not ridicule. So I just went on teasing you, praying all the time that you would act on all my hints. Damn you, Eddie. You never did."

Nick started to cry and buried his head in his hands.

I got up and sat down next to him on his lounge chair. I removed his hands from his head and held them in mine. "Idiot," I said. "I'm crazy in love with you. I was afraid that if I responded to your hints and you weren't serious, you might sock me into kingdom come. So I decided to be content just to be near you, and be your friend if you would let me. I want you so badly, and to find out that you feel the same way, well, I can't believe it."

Suddenly I had a terrible thought. "You're still not playing with me, are you?" I asked Nick fearfully.

Nick could only shake his head. He was crying.

"How would you like me to be your trainer tonight?" I asked him. He didn't answer, but got up and led me to his bedroom.

"I'll start with the basics," I said, mimicking Nick's training manners. And I did. First I showed him how to suck cock. I demonstrated on him and after only three strokes he nearly came so I stopped, and then I generously let him practice on me. When I felt he had the knack, I asked him to get out the lube that he told me he used to whack off with. I showed him how to grease my ass, and insert a finger or two to get me ready. I lay on my back, wrapped my legs around his waist and guided him into me. I told him to start pumping just as he would a vagina, and he did.

"No way is this like a vagina," he said. This is so fucking tight and hot. Oh, I'm coming. Should I pull out?"

"Not on your life. Let her rip." He came in several pumping streams, screaming loudly all the while. I could feel myself filling up and some of his cum was dripping out on the bed sheets. It's a good thing Marla wouldn't be home for a few days. When he was done spurting, he collapsed on me. I found his lips and started to kiss him gently. I wanted to see his reaction. He kissed me back. Hard! He parted my lips and let our tongues have a wrestling match. He was responding like he had been gay all of his life.

He said, "Fuck me now." It sounded like a military command.

"No," I said, "I'm too big. We'll have to work on you first and get you ready, but I promise you'll have the pleasure. I have to get something at home. I'll be right back." I jumped out of bed, wrapped a towel around me and ran next door through our back yards. I was back in seconds with two dildoes and another tube of lube. One dildo was a little smaller than Nick's cock and one was almost as big as mine.

I began to lube his ass. When I inserted one finger he took it easily and even told me how good it felt. The second finger went in almost as easily, but he resisted the third finger. I begged him to relax, that I would never hurt him, and that even if it took weeks to get him ready, I promised him that it would be worth it. That did the trick. He relaxed and eventually I was able to insert four fingers. I left them in for a while and found his prostate which I began to massage. "Oh that feels so wonderful," he murmured in pleasure.

"You like my massage better than yours?" I asked.

All I got back was, "MMMMM."

He was doing so well, I decided to ignore the smaller dildo and go for broke. I removed my fingers from his ass, lubed up the larger dildo and placed the head at his crack. His ass began to pull the dildo inside him. I realized that Nick was actually sucking it up. I had to be patient and work hard to get past the sphincter. Nick was eager and really trying to help and before long we had penetrated his point of resistance. Now I inserted the dildo slowly. Every so often Nick winced in pain. I would stop pushing and when he got used to it I would push again. When it was all in, I let him rest for a bit and then began pumping and rotating. I made sure his prostate was getting a pleasurable work out.

"Please," he begged me, "stop before I come again. I want the real thing."

Who was I to argue with this hunk of a man? Out came the dildo. My lubed and throbbing cock was ready for action. Nick was a natural. I went in slowly, but he was all slicked up and I met little resistance. I started pumping slowly, and in very short strokes, until Nick began yelling for me to go harder. His command turned me into a beast. I began to pump long and vigorous strokes as quickly as I could. Suddenly Nick screamed and shot another load up his abdomen, stomach and face. Some of his cum landed on his lips and damned if he didn't flick his tongue and taste it. When he came, his ass constricted on my cock and as I yelled, "I'm cumming," I shot copiously into his waiting hole.

"My God, that feels so good," he said. "It's so warm and wet. Why didn't you tell me that sex with a guy was this great?"

"You never asked, cock teaser."

We lay still for a while, me on top of him. Without regard to the mess we had made, we rolled over on our backs and using my fingers, I devoured the rest of his cum from his beautiful body. When he saw what I was doing he joined in with me. Finally, we rolled over on our sides facing each other. We fondled our cocks and kissed passionately. I came up for air and finally said, "I love you Nick, but there's something we can't ignore, and that's Marla. We've got to talk about her."

Nick sat up in bed, and shocked me by roaring with laughter. "There is no Marla," he said. There hasn't been a Marla for several days. The bitch ran off with her boss, and I couldn't be happier. I won't have to pay alimony, the house is in my name, and I get to spend the rest of my life with someone I really love. You!" He began kissing me so that I could hardly breathe. He rolled on top of me, and as much as I wanted to say something, I couldn't. His lips were pressed so tightly on mine, that I was literally speechless.

I had finally conquered my fear of relationships, thanks to Nick's seduction. I suddenly realized that if Nick had not teased me for so long, I would never have reached this point of completely wanting to be his. I might have settled for yet another fuck buddy relationship.

As we lay there kissing, with our cocks pressed together, I could only thank whatever angels had maneuvered fate to bring us together.

"Thank you! Thank you! Thank you!" I screamed out loud, and Nick laughed at me.

THE CYCLE OF LOVE

Part One - Boy Meets Boy (1950)

It was hard to say who was more frightened. They were both one day past their eighteenth birthdays. Joe was from Manhattan and Kurt was from Peoria. They had arrived at the train station in Chicago on separate trains and were instructed to look for a chief petty officer, who would take them on an escorted bus to Great Lakes Naval Training Station. Neither had any idea how many other guys would be joining them.

Joe spotted Chief Martin first. He was standing in the main terminal holding a placard reading "Great Lakes." He approached him, but didn't know exactly what to say. The Chief spoke first. "Name?" he asked.

"Joe Carlone," he answered. The chief searched a paper fastened to a clipboard, and made a check mark.

"Join those other recruits over there, Joseph," he said, as his head nodded toward a group of equally scared boys huddled together about ten feet from where he now stood. Joe added himself to the group, and nodded at no one in particular as he blended in. Nobody in the pack was talking.

About five minutes later Kurt joined the group. He was scared to death, but he was also a pretty friendly country boy. Joe was standing closest to him. Kurt thrust his hand at Joe and said, "Hi, I'm Kurt Carlson. Pleased to meet you."

Actually Joe was relieved that someone had broken the ice. He returned Kurt's handshake, and almost immediately everyone was shaking hands and making introductions. Within an hour, there were fifty of them. The Chief approached and asked for attention.

"There are two buses waiting outside the terminal. I want you to assemble curbside. When I call your name, I want you to enter the bus you are assigned to and start filling it from the rear. Move it!"

They all rushed outside. All any of them had with them was a small toiletry kit which they had been instructed to fill with a toothbrush, toothpaste, a razor and shaving cream.

"We'll start with bus one," Chief Martin instructed the youths. "Abrams, Arthur, Atkins, Bates, Beck, Brooks, Carlone, Carlson..." He continued until each bus was full. Joe and Kurt ended up sharing a seat on the way to the naval base. Because everything was assigned alphabetically, they shared an upper and a lower bunk as well in the fifty man barracks which was to be their home for ninety days, and the home of Company C.

Joe hardly spoke on the way to the base. He kept looking out the window at the rural scenery, which he saw precious little of in New York. Kurt just kept yakking away about life on the farm, his parents, his sisters, his high school chums. Finally he said to Joe, "Tell me about you."

"What's to tell? I barely made it through high school. My dad OD'd last year. I'm the youngest in my family. My two brothers were long gone when my dad died, God knows where, and my mom couldn't feed the two of us, so I joined up."

"Wow, I'm sorry," Kurt said.

"Why? It's no skin off your teeth. Besides, now I'll get my three squares and I won't have to steal. I wasn't cut out for that street gang stuff." Joe brushed off Kurt's sympathy.

The weeks flew by quickly. Their days were filled with marching drills (with and without rifles), calisthenics (with and without rifles), body building, swimming classes, rifle practice, fire fighting, boxing, and whatever else was going to make them into able bodied seamen. Joe and Kurt became friends to the whole company, but their own friendship was the closest. They shared a bed, so to speak, and they sat next to each other in every class. They even marched side by side, thanks to their names.

As their boot camp days progressed, Joe turned at least ten pounds of fat into ten pounds of muscle. Kurt gained another twelve pounds, all of it muscle. They kept telling each other how great they both looked.

Half way through the training, they were given a six hour pass. It was part of the training, and was designed to teach the recruits how to get back to base within the allotted time.

The two boys donned their dress blues, added spit to their already shiny black shoes, and admired how great they looked in Uncle Sam's uniforms. As soon as they left the base, they cocked their sailor hats at a precarious angle. It was far from regulation, but they both looked quite dapper and handsome.

Time was short so they took the train from the base to the nearest city, Waukegan, IL. They strolled along the street nearest the train station and found a small restaurant. They each had a cheeseburger and a milkshake for lunch. The cheeseburger was disappointing. It was greasy and fatty, but the milkshake was like nectar to the two sailors. When they finished lunch, they started to stroll back to the train station. They had plenty of time, but they decided to take the first train back to the base anyway.

When they reached the station, there was nobody else on the platform. They sat down on a bench to await the train. As they sat down their hands accidently touched as they placed them on the seat. Joe's first impulse was to pull away, but he decided not to. Why draw attention to a little accident? Kurt didn't seem very anxious to change the situation either.

They sat silently until Joe said, "I gotta take a leak. I'll be right back." As he stood up, Kurt did the same.

"I need to go too," Kurt said, and they went to find the men's room. Now both boys had seen each other naked in the showers, and more than once they had peed and even shit next to each other, but somehow doing it here in a public place outside the base, was a little awkward for both of them.

As they were peeing side by side, Joe started to laugh.

"What's so funny?" Kurt asked.

"I haven't whacked off since I left home. I'm afraid of getting caught, and I am so horny," Joe explained.

"Me too," Kurt agreed. "Why don't you go into a stall and do it. I'll keep watch, and then you can do that for me".

"Why not?" Joe answered. He finished peeing, and never tucking his cock back in, he headed for the stall. Kurt could not help but notice that his buddy was rock hard. As soon as Joe closed the stall door, Kurt looked around. The bathroom had a lock on the door and he walked over and engaged the lock. What the hell. Then he yelled to Joe, "Don't be nervous, friend, I locked the door."

Kurt was picturing what was happening behind the door and he took his cock out and started stroking it. He had never been with a girl. His preference was always for other boys, but he had successfully suppressed it and so he was still a virgin. As he got near his climax, he began to fantasize sucking Joe's cock. The idea scared him so much that he stopped jerking off and returned his fast shrinking cock into his pants.

He realized that Joe wasn't done yet, but he had nearly cum. He called through the booth, "What's taking so long?"

"I don't know. Come in here, would you." Kurt's heart began to pound. He had no time to digest what Joe had said and he opened the door. Joe was whacking away, but his cock was soft compared to a few minutes ago.

"Jerk off with me," he said, "like a circle jerk. I'm used to those. It will help." Kurt didn't need to be told twice. He whipped out his cock which was hardening once again.

"Wait," Joe said, and he handed Kurt a wad of toilet paper. "Catch your spunk in this so you don't get dirty." Kurt took the wad of paper in his left hand and resumed jerking off. The two boys stared steadily at each other, Joe seated on the toilet seat, and Kurt standing facing him. Only when he found himself reaching the end, did Kurt close his eyes and let loose. When he opened his eyes, Joe was still at it, but he could tell that he was getting close. Without giving it a thought, he pushed Joe's hand away from his cock and he started to whack his buddy off. Joe was happy to let him. He slid down a bit more on the toilet seat and began to moan. His eyes rolled up in his head and with a stifled scream, he came. Joe had remembered the wad of paper in his hand and put it over his cock head just in time to keep from splattering both of them.

They did nothing for a moment and then Joe said, "Give me your paper." Trance like, Kurt obeyed Joe's request. Joe threw both wads into the toilet and flushed them down. They both began to dress and finally Kurt said with a sob, "I'm really sorry, Joe. I don't know what came over me."

"Why are you sorry? That was simply the greatest." He turned toward Kurt and kissed him on the lips. Kurt was startled but regained his composure quickly. He kissed back hard, until their lips parted and their tongues began to slide over each other.

Kurt said, "Don't hate me and please don't turn me in, but I have always thought I was gay and I know I love you."

Joe kissed Kurt harder. "Me too," he murmured.

When they left the bathroom, the platform was still empty, but a few minutes later they were joined by a few other young men from their company.

Early in their training, they had been asked to name their preference for specialized training after boot camp. Neither Joe nor Kurt had any thoughts on what they wanted to do, so they left the card blank. Consequently they were assigned to whatever was available. Both sat expectantly in their seats as Chief Martin read their assignments. Kurt was going to Yeoman's school in San Diego and Joe was remaining here at Great Lakes to attend Hospital Corps School. Neither was disappointed. Joe was actually thrilled. Hospital Corpsmen were often reassigned to the Marine Corps. If he was transferred to the Marines, that would be really cool.

Then they realized that they would be separated by nearly half a continent. Their joy was short lived.

Part Two - Boy Loses Boy

The members of the company received a two week leave before reporting to their next assignments. Joe had no place to go and Kurt begged him to come home with him. "I spoke to my folks and they would love it," he assured Joe.

I've never been on a farm," he told Kurt as if Kurt didn't know. "Do you really fuck sheep?"

Kurt groaned and socked Joe on the arm.

The Carsons were very hospitable and Kurt's two younger sisters flirted with Joe the entire time he was there. He could have had either of the farmer's daughters, but he had his eye on the farmer's son. The boys both shared Kurt's room which only had a three quarter size mattress.

The innocent Carsons never dreamed that anything improper could occur so they apologized to Joe that they couldn't offer him a room of his own or at least a larger bed. They did call around to see if any of their neighbors had a cot, but they were unsuccessful.

The first night, the boys went to bed in their skivvies. "Let's do it again," Kurt whispered as his lips brushed against Joe's.

"We can do better than that," Joe said. Before Kurt knew what was happening, Joe pulled Kurt's underwear down and pulled it off his ankles.

"What did you have in mind?" Kurt asked seductively.

"Let me show you," Joe said. He leaned over Kurt and began to suckle his nipples. Kurt purred like a kitten. Then Joe went down further and drove his tongue into Kurt's innie. Finally he started to lick Kurt's inner thighs and his balls. He sucked the sweet spot between Kurt's crack and his balls, lingering there quite awhile. At last, he started to lick Kurt's rock hard shaft. He rolled his tongue all over Kurt's cockhead and parted his piss slit with his tongue. Kurt was rolling back and forth on the bed. Then it happened. Joe took Kurt's seven inch, uncut cock slowly into his mouth. He took as much as he could and started sucking away. He couldn't believe how good it tasted, and Kurt could not believe how good it felt.

Suddenly Kurt pushed his fist into his mouth and came. Spurt after spurt invaded Joe's mouth. Joe was pleased at how good it tasted and he just kept swallowing until it was all gone, and Kurt began to shrink.

"That was awesome," Kurt said. "You've done this many times before, haven't you?"

"I swear this is the first time. Ever since you whacked me off, I have practiced in my head just what I would do to you if we were ever fortunate enough to have sex together. You benefitted from my imagination."

Kurt rolled over Joe and began kissing him. "Let me show you what I dreamed of doing." He started with Joe's mouth, kissing him sensuously. Down he moved, to Joe's neck, nipples and navel. Joe thought Kurt would now go down and hit pay dirt, but instead he rolled Joe over. His tongue wandered up and down Joe's back and reached his bubbly ass. Kurt squeezed and kissed Joe's cheeks. Then he parted them and ran his tongue up and down Joe's crack. At strategic moments, he inserted his tongue. It thrilled Kurt to hear Joe sighing with pleasure.

"You're torturing me," Joe said, so Kurt turned him over and went down on Joe's waiting cock.

"Save some of the juice for me," Joe said. "It tastes so good."

Mr. Carson knocked loudly on their door the next morning before dawn and roused them both. The two lads were expected to help on the farm during their stay. The pair was so healthy and fit, that they finished their chores early and had a good deal of the day to themselves. Kurt's father was amazed at how strong and muscular his son had become in three short months. He was so proud of him.

They rose so early on the farm that showers were taken at night. Joe showered before Kurt and when Kurt came into their room and closed the door behind him, he had something in the pocket of his robe. He pulled out a jar of petroleum jelly and announced to Joe that tonight was their big night.

"You can fuck me first," he told Joe. He lay down on his back and raised his legs exposing his asshole. He handed the jar to Joe and said, "Grease me good, lover." Joe applied the jelly to two of his fingers and inserted both gently into Kurt's crack.

"Awesome!" Kurt croaked. Encouraged by Kurt's reaction, Joe greased his cock, placed it at Kurt's hole and began to push gently. Kurt flinched and Joe stopped abruptly. Kurt could not talk. He wrapped his legs around Joe's ass and pushed him in slowly. Joe's head went past the sphincter and suddenly he sank all the way in.

"Don't move yet," Kurt pleaded. "Let's enjoy the moment." Nature isn't so patient, and involuntarily they both began the dance of love. Joe was able to stop himself twice from cumming, but eventually he had to let loose. His jism filled Kurt's hole and some of it began to drip out. When Joe's cock shrunk and fell out, Joe scooped up the spunk on Kurt's ass and they both feasted on it.

"Have I told you how much I love you?" Joe asked Kurt.

"No, but you can show me." Kurt began to lubricate Joe's ass.

Never did time go faster for either of them. They promised to write to each other every day. At night they cried together in contemplation of the inevitable. The morning came for departure. Joe kissed Mrs. Carson and Kurt's two sisters goodbye, and Mr. Carson drove him and Kurt to the train station. He and Kurt could not show their affection at the station and had said their goodbyes the night before.

They would be together until Chicago. Then Joe would take the train to the naval base and Kurt would take a cab to the airport to board his flight to San Diego. On the train they held hands under a blanket and occasionally fondled each other. Both sets of eyes were moist with tears.

Part Three - Boy Finds Boy (1950-1959)

At first they wrote to each other daily, then once or twice a week, then occasionally, and then not at all. If life was a romance novel, this would not have happened, but life is reality. It's difficult to stay in love when there is so much distance between you, especially when there are so many other hot bodies surrounding you.

Kurt finished his school and remained in San Diego at the naval base. After a year he was assigned duty on an aircraft carrier. He concluded his hitch on that ship and after discharge he returned to the farm which would be all his very shortly. He would regret it in years to come, but he married one of his high school girlfriends. They had two children, but eventually she started cheating on Kurt. Kurt took full responsibility, because he hardly ever touched her. They divorced five years after they married.

When Joe finished school, he was assigned to the naval hospital in Philadelphia, PA. He remained there for a few months and then he was deployed overseas and was transferred to the First Marine Division. He saw almost a year of combat duty in Korea. From there he went to the naval hospital in Yokosuka, Japan. He was discharged from there.

He returned to New York and located his mother. She had remarried and was doing just fine. Using the GI Bill and all the money he had squirreled away while he served in the navy, he enrolled in nursing school at NYU.

The first day there he met Tony. Tony was just out of high school. He had just turned eighteen, and had never served in any of the armed forces. They were the only two males in the class and so they bunked together, and became good friends. They had little time for recreation and studied long hours together.

One day, Joe said, "We are getting real stale. We need a break. What do you say we take a night off and just relax at some bar?"

"It sounds like a plan to me," Tony said. "Do you have a place in mind?"

"Actually I do. It's called The Hot Spot."

Tony started to laugh. "I know that place well. It's my favorite gay bar."

"Mine too," Joe agreed. "Why didn't you tell me you were gay?"

"You never asked," Tony said, "and I'm not in the habit of outing myself."

They went to the bar that night and Tony introduced Joe to some of his friends who were there, and Joe introduced Tony to some of his. They had a couple of drinks and then began to dance. It was in the days before disco took over the gay bars. The music at this time was slow and romantic, and when you danced you actually touched your partner.

The dance floor was crowded and the two nursing students were crammed together. It didn't take too much imagination for Joe to feel Tony's hardon rubbing against him. That got him going and before long he was grinding against Tony. Moved by the romantic music, they kissed, really without knowing they were doing it. They kissed over and over again.

Tony put his hands on Joe's ass and pushed him harder against him. "I think I'd like to go home," he said.

It is honest to say that at first they were only fuck buddies. But little by little they realized that neither wanted to be with anyone else. Even when they weren't having sex, they would have fun together. They enjoyed being together, studying together, eating together, going to movies and plays together. If they were apart, they were at loose ends. They found themselves yearning for each other.

One evening, Joe returned to their dorm room after having had dinner at his mother's apartment. When he opened the door, he found Tony crying.

"What's the matter?" Joe asked and swooped Tony into his arms.

"We're the matter," Tony wailed. "I don't want you to go to your mother without me, and I don't want to visit my folks without you. I can't stand doing things and going places without you. I want us to be a couple. I love you, dammit. I'm half a person without you. I'm useless without you. Pity me!"

All the while he was wailing, Joe's arms were wrapped around him. "Jerk," Joe said, "I love you too. I made up my mind months ago that you and I were for life."

Mimicking the old silent movie heroes he said to Tony, "Kiss me, fool!!! And when you are through kissing me, I'd be much obliged if you would fuck me or vice versa."

"Your wish is my command," Tony said, continuing to play a part in an old movie.

It is safe to say that Joe never thought of Kurt again. He could hardly remember him. Not so for Kurt. He constantly thought of Joe and his lost love. Every time he whacked off, Joe was his fantasy lover. He never found anyone else to fill the void in his life.

THE SECRET LIFE OF A COP

Part One

Let's start with Tom (Thomas Connelly). He's twenty-eight years old; tall, blond and handsome; a police officer with the West Palm Beach, FL police department; a very tough cop; married to Maureen; has never cheated on her; has two sons aged four and one; lives in suburban West Palm Beach at 2020 Commodore Circle; favorite sport is baseball; plays on a police hard ball team; his best friend, and patrol car partner, is Luke.

Now let's talk about Luke (Lucas Demetrius). He's twenty-seven years old; tall, dark and handsome; a police officer with the West Palm Beach, FL police department; a very tough cop; married to Emily: has never cheated on her; has one daughter aged three; lives in suburban West Palm Beach at 2021 Commodore Circle; favorite sport is baseball; plays on a police hard ball team; his best friend, and patrol car partner, is Tom.

When they are not working, tending the lawn or minding the children, they each stand in front of their homes, which are directly across the street from one another, and toss a baseball across the road. That's really not quite accurate.

Tossing conjures up a vision of an easy lob. Their goal is to throw the ball so fast and so hard that one day the catcher will not be able to catch it in his well oiled mitt. So far neither has been successful, and each really hopes they never will be. Sometimes, even through the mitt, the palm of their hand is red and sore after the pitching. They are both in great physical condition and they are very strong.

Tom's in-laws live in Tampa, FL and Luke's in-laws live in Queens, NY. At least twice a year, each of the wives takes a week or two off and visits her parents with the kids. When Tom's wife is away, he is expected every evening for dinner at Luke's. When Luke's wife is away, he is expected every evening for dinner at Tom's. It's a given. There are no formal invitations issued. None are necessary. After all, these two guys lay their lives on the line as a team every single day of the week.

Every Saturday night, if the men are not working, the women get a baby sitter and they go out together. Sometimes, it's just a movie, sometimes it's just dinner, sometimes it's dinner and a movie. Once or twice a year, it's a Broadway musical at the Kravis Center for the Performing Arts. None of them drink, and they rarely visit any local bars.

The men have each received several commendations for their heroic police work. More importantly, they volunteer at local boys' clubs and coach baseball and soccer in their spare time. Both are true heroes and role models in their community. All the kids look up to them, and aspire to be just like them when they grow up.

The caption on their pictures would more than likely read: "All American Hero" so no matter what you read from here on in, they will always be true all American heroes. I am about to reveal a very private secret and it won't change who they are or what they represent.

Let me inform you that Tom has a tiny little secret. He is gay, but he doesn't know it for a fact. He has not gone beyond voyeurism. So far he has limited his activity to reading gay porn on the internet and entering gay chat rooms. He himself does not chat, but reads everybody else's postings. So far, this big, strapping, macho man hasn't had the courage to post a comment of his own, or to go any further than that. His biggest challenge is keeping his secret from Luke. He is consumed with lust for his work partner.

His most difficult moments are when he is alone with Luke in their patrol car or in the showers after a baseball game. He must control himself from wanting to pull Luke to him, kissing his lips, sucking his cock, or shoving Luke's cock up his ass. It is pure torture for him, but so far Luke does not suspect that Tom is in love with him.

Maureen is often too tired after a day with the kids to offer him sex, and if she does, she has a 'let's get it over with' attitude. So Tom masturbates a lot. When he is whacking off, he fantasizes he is with a man, doing some of the things he has read about or seen on the male porn sites. It doesn't seem to bother him in the least that he is fantasizing having sex with a man. It's an easy secret to keep to himself, and from his best friend Luke, so far.

Often when Maureen has told him that she is too tired for sex, Tom goes into his den to go online. He not only closes the door, but he locks it. He has a secret screen name and a secret password that he hopes Maureen could never guess. Even though Tom's cut cock is an average six inches hard, his secret screen name is 'Wellhung.' His secret password is 'Policebiz.'

Once on line, he enters his favorite chat room: 'Twenty Something in WPB, FL.' He scans the list of screen names of the people who are chatting in the room. If he thinks a screen name is particularly enticing or particularly interesting, he clicks on that name and then brings up that person's profile. He has often been tempted to contact some of them, but he always chickens out. He wants to experience male sex so badly that it hurts, but he is scared to death to pursue it further.

One night he entered the chat room and was attracted to one of the screen names in the chat room, because it was almost like his own. He clicked on 'Hungwell.' Then he went to Hungwell's profile:

Age: mid twenties; (Reality Check: 27)

Height: 6'1"; (Reality Check: 6'1")

Weight: 185 lbs; (Reality Check: 200 lbs.)

Hobbies: Pleasing my man; (Reality Check: Has never been with a man)

Motto: I've never met a man I didn't like.

Tom found the profile to be pretty standard, but he was more intrigued by the screen name. He entered the chat room, clicked on Hungwell, screwed up his courage and sent him an IM.

Part Two

Wellhung: Hi Hungwell. How goes it?

Hungwell: Hi Wellhung. How goes it with you? Interesting screen name!

Tom's heart began to beat overtime. He never expected a reply and he was extremely nervous. He had no idea what to say. Before he could answer, he got another IM from Hungwell.

Hungwell: I just read your profile. You sound like you're me.

Wellhung: I know. Ain't it a hoot?

Hungwell: Are you really mid twenties?

Wellhung: 28

Hungwell: 27 here, really 6'1", 200 lbs. Sorry

Wellhung: No problem. I'm 6'2" and 210. I guess we both need a gym.

Hungwell: You sound like a nice guy.

Wellhung: I am. You sound nice too.

Hungwell: Everybody says so.

Wellhung: What's your favorite thing to do?

Hungwell: Play sports.

Wellhung: I mean sexually.

Hungwell: Sorry. I'm new at this.

Wellhung: Me too.

Hungwell: Are you as scared as I am?

Wellhung: Yes, I'm scared too.

Hungwell: I'd like to try some man sex sometime, but to be honest, I'm married and I'm not sure about this.

Wellhung: Bingo. I'm married too. Scared shitless, but horny, curious and if I can get some courage, I'd like to try it with a dude sometime also. Need someone who has to be as discreet as I have to be.

Hungwell: Right.

Wellhung: This IMing shit is hard to do. Can I E-mail you sometime? Then I can think about what I want to say, and we can get better acquainted.

Hungwell: Great idea. Let's get to know each other by being pen pals first. Maybe there's a future here. I've been pining for a long time.

Wellhung: Me too. I'm signing off now and going to my E-Mail. Ciao.

Hungwell: Ciao.

To: Hungwell@aol.com

From: Wellhung@aol.com

Subject: Getting to Know You

Time: 11:02 PM Tuesday Jul. 14

Hi Hungwell. It was nice chatting with you this evening. Here goes. I'm going to let it all hang out (no sexual innuendo intended). I'm happily married with kids, but I have been wondering what it would be like to have sex with a man for as long as I can remember. When I jerk off, I fantasize I'm playing 69 with some one who looks like Rock Hudson or Brad Pitt. Sometimes I get really bad and imagine that Rock or Brad is fucking me or I'm fucking one of them. I'm curious about how all that would feel, but right now I'm curious to know if you have similar feelings. I must tell you that I am surprised that I feel comfortable sharing this with you. Maybe it's because we are in the same boat, but probably it's because you're anonymous. Wellhung.

Tom re-read the note, and did not hesitate to click on send. He decided to wait ten minutes to see if Hungwell would answer him. While waiting, he returned to the chat room and was pleased to note that Hungwell was not in the room. He hoped he was still on line and was writing to him. He added Hungwell to his buddy list and it indicated that he was indeed on line.

After a little while he heard the little bell indicating he had an E-Mail coming in.

To: Wellhung@aol.com

From: Hungwell@aol.com

Subject: Getting to Know You

Time: 11:18 PM Tuesday Jul.14

Hi Buddy: There's nothing you can tell me and no emotion you can feel that I haven't known and felt. You already know that I am married; we both are. But the desire to be with a man is consuming me. My wife never gives me head. She thinks it's dirty. Talking of dirty, I long to stick my cock up some hairy, dirty ass hole and then have the guy fuck me right back. I keep imagining that the feeling of being filled up in your gut must be so sexually electrifying. Who better than another man can know and feel what you are longing for? A woman sleeps with you because it's her marital duty. I sometimes wonder if there are any women who really enjoy sex with a man. Not from the way my buddies talk at work. I'll bet most women would rather be with another woman for the same reason I'd rather be with a man. I hope you won't think I'm being too forward talking like this, but like you said, I feel comfortable sharing this with you. Also, it is really a wonder that I have found someone who understands and isn't judging me. My best, Hungwell

Tom did not hesitate to answer back.

To: Hungwell@aol.com

From: Wellhung@aol.com

Subject: Getting to Know You

Time: 11:48 PM, Tuesday, Jul. 14

Dear friend: Funny you should say that about judging someone. A wise man once told me that we can have thousands of friends, but we cannot consider ourselves to be lucky unless we can find one special person to whom we can reveal our innermost secrets, without fear of being judged, and with the certainty that we will still be friends after we have poured out our hearts. He told me to find that someone and I would find a true friend. The rest are mere acquaintances. I know this is crazy. We just met, but already I have told you, and you have told me, that one tremendous secret that haunts both of us. Are we still friends? I think so. Are you judging me? I think not. Have I found that one special friend? I hope so. I have tried a hundred times to confide in my best friend, but I couldn't even tell him what I have just revealed to you. I think it would end our friendship. So I guess that demotes him to a mere acquaintance. I would like to continue our conversation, but I hear my wife stirring. She may be looking for me. I promise to write again as soon as possible. From my heart. Wellhung.

The next day, Tom told Luke to drive the patrol car. Luke could tell that his friend was pre-occupied and was glad to help him out. Tom just couldn't get Hungwell out of his mind.

"What's wrong, buddy?" Luke wanted to know.

Tom thought, 'That's what Hungwell called me, buddy.' "Nothing's wrong," Tom answered. I've just got a lot on my mind. I'll be fine. Hell, I am fine." Suddenly Tom was his old self again. Tonight he would write to Hungwell, but he couldn't make time go faster so he might as well land back on earth. After all, his job required his total focus and concentration.

Tom couldn't wait for Maureen's bedtime, so after dinner, he told her that he had some important paper work to do. He went into the den and locked the door. It was still summer and light outside. Luke happened to call to see if he wanted to pitch a few balls, but he declined. Now Luke was sure that his buddy had some problem. He determined to find out what was bothering him.

Tom logged on with his dial up connection and vowed to switch to DSL. Finally (it seemed forever) he reached his E-Mail. There was a letter from Hungwell which was written after Tom had signed off the night before.

Hello dear friend, I agree with your definition of true friendship. Since you are the only person in the world who knows my secret and you haven't labeled me faggot or given up on our budding friendship, I guess we are real friends. I feel good about that. You got me thinking about someone who I have always felt was my best friend in the world. I started to ask myself what would happen if I told him my secret, and I shuddered at the thought. There is no doubt in my mind that the friendship would end. That would be devastating to me, so I will keep my secret from him. Ciao, good buddy, Hungwell.

Tom hit the reply button.

I could hardly work today, thinking about you. Believe it or not, I didn't think about having sex with you, although that would be nice. I thought of you as being my friend. I couldn't wait to get to the computer and write to you, my friend. I wanted so desperately to talk to you and share more of myself with you. Can I call you sometime? Do you see us meeting in the near future? Love, Wellhung.

Hungwell answered about an hour later and Tom was visibly upset.

You are moving way too fast for me. I already cherish our friendship, but I am still not sure if I could have sex with a man. If we were to meet, even for a cup of coffee, I am afraid it might go further. I don't want to do something I will regret later on. Hungwell

Tom answered:

Dear friend: You are so right, and I do apologize. I don't want to lose your friendship. No more pressure, I promise you. Let's just correspond. If you reach a point where you think you would like to meet me, I'll be ready. Your friend, Wellhung.

Tom wrote to Hungwell several more times but received no answer. He was really distraught. He went to the chat room every night, but Hungwell was not there. He chided himself for having rushed things. He was so distracted at work that Luke threatened to request a different partner. His appetite was so shot that he lost a ton of weight. All his uniforms needed altering.

Luke kept begging his friend to tell him what was wrong, but Tom said he couldn't tell him, that he wouldn't understand. Luke grew angry. "If we are real friends," he said, "you can tell me anything."

Tom's heart skipped a beat when he heard that. Could he really tell Luke the truth? Would he be judgmental? Would they still be friends? He knew he could not say anything, and turned away from Luke's friendship.

When it seemed he could not sink lower, and Luke was ready to make good on his promise to get a new partner, Tom received an E-Mail from Hungwell.

Dear Wellhung. I am sorry I haven't written. To tell the truth, I was trying to get you out of my system. As you can see I have had no success. I have missed your notes (and your friendship) more than I can put into words. As for the sex part, I have been whacking off constantly and fantasizing that you and I are doing some pretty nasty (and wonderful) things together. I guess what I am saying is, yes I am ready to meet you if you still want to meet me. Maybe we'll love each other and jump right into bed. Maybe we'll hate each other and that will be the end of it. Even if it's the end, I am ready to confide in you that I won't stop looking for a man to have sex with. It's all I think about. I believe I am possessed and the devil won't leave me until I do it. I'll leave it to you to set the time and place to meet. Love, Hungwell.

Tom was shocked at his reaction to the E-Mail. He started to cry. He hadn't cried since he was a kid. He might have been crying but he felt like a million bucks. There was still enough light out to play some ball. He called Luke and told him to step outside with his mitt. He was challenging him to catch his fast balls.

Luke was delighted and ran outside so fast, he got out before Tom. They could only play for about twenty minutes when it got too dark to see. When the game was over, Luke crossed the street and did something he had never done to Tom before. He embraced him in a bear hug and whispered in his ear, "Welcome home, buddy."

That night after Maureen fell asleep, Tom ran to the computer. His buddy list indicated that Hungwell was on line. Instead of going to E-Mail Tom sent him an IM.

Wellhung: Hello dear friend.

Hungwell: Hello to you, buddy.

Wellhung: I've picked a place to meet. It's very public so one of us or both of us can bolt out, if it should go that way.

Hungwell: I have a feeling it will go well. Where shall we meet?

Wellhung: Can you make it Saturday morning at 11AM. I'll create a chore I have to handle.

Hungwell: I can do that. Where?

Wellhung: How about City Place in front of Starbucks. I'll meet you out front.

Hungwell: How will I know you?

Wellhung: I'll carry a black attaché case. It's Saturday. I don't think there will be many guys toting a business bag wearing shorts. I'm 6'2" and blond. That should help. How shall I know you?

Hungwell: Don't worry. I'll look for a tall blond wearing shorts and toting an attaché case. I can't wait. See you there. Ciao.

Tom had three whole days to wait, and time never went slower. Luke was amazed at the change in him, but was willing to accept this good turn of events without questioning it.

On Saturday morning Tom told Maureen he was way behind in his paper work and had to go down to the station to catch up. He left the house carrying an attaché case. He got to City Place and was parked in the parking ramp an hour before meeting time. At first he wanted to go wait in front of Starbucks but he was afraid that if Hungwell saw him and didn't like what he saw, he might run. He decided to get to Starbucks promptly at 11AM. Coincidentally, Hungwell reasoned the same way. Both of them were sitting in their cars waiting for time to pass. They were at opposite ends of the parking ramp.

At 10:55AM each of them got out of their cars and started toward Starbucks. Tom's heart beat was at a dangerous pitch. They didn't know it, but they were walking toward each other. Suddenly Hungwell saw a black attaché case being carried by a tall blond man wearing shorts and walking toward him. He stopped dead in his tracks and would have run, but Tom had already seen him and he too stopped cold. There was no way they could run from each other so they continued to approach one another. Tom looked into Hungwell's dark eyes and asked, "Hungwell?"

"Yes, and you must be Wellhung."

Tom placed the attaché case on the ground and embraced Hungwell. "Oh my God," he said. "Luke, it's you. Oh Luke, no wonder I fell in love so fast."

"We should be ashamed," Luke said.

"Sorry, man, but I refuse to be ashamed of loving you," Tom reacted.

"Not that," Luke corrected him. "I was thinking about what you said was the true mark of friendship. We didn't trust each other enough to tell the truth. That will never happen again."

"Amen," Tom agreed.

"Where can we go to be alone?" Luke asked.

"Can you wait until tomorrow? Maureen is going to Tampa for two weeks with the kids. Naturally, I'll have dinner at your house. We'll toss the ball around a little, and then we'll tell Emily you are going over to my place to shoot some pool. What happens then is that a whole lot of fantasies are going to come true."

They went into Starbucks, ordered coffee and found a quiet table. For almost two hours they did what they both had wanted to do for years but feared the results. They poured their hearts out, telling each other how much love they felt toward one another, and how their secret yearnings tortured them.

The next day went as planned. Maureen loaded up her mini van, strapped in the boys, kissed Tom goodbye, a chaste peck on the lips, and left. During the day Tom and Luke did yard maintenance chores, but the afternoon tropical sun cut it short. They each showered and put on sweet smelling fresh clothes; shorts and tank tops.

Tom hung out at Luke's the rest of the afternoon, watching some old movies on TV. He whispered to Tom that he had some male porn videos to watch later. He had confiscated them in a vice sting. He figured that they both needed some instructions. When it came close to dinner, they helped Emily set the table.

After dinner, they played catch for a while, a very short while, and told Emily that they would be at Tom's playing pool. They rushed into the house and headed for Tom's bedroom. They shed their skimpy clothing as quickly as possible and jumped into bed. They faced each other and wrapped their arms around one another. Their erections were pressed hard against one another.

"How great is this?" Tom asked. "Shall I put on one of the tapes?"

'Nah," Luke answered, "I think we are men enough to know what to do. Just tell me you have lube in the house. You promised to make my fantasies come true."

They started by playing sixty-nine. At some critical point, Luke interrupted and told Tom that as much as he wanted Tom to come inside his ass, this was too good to stop doing. He wanted to continue sucking until they both came. "After all," he said, "we have a life time to experiment with everything else our bodies have to offer one another." With that he resumed sucking Tom and Tom resumed sucking Luke. They came almost simultaneously, and surprised each other by swallowing whatever was offered to them. Later they both agreed that it tasted like honey. Luke said that it only tasted like honey because it came from his honey. They lay wrapped up in one another's arms for some time. They kissed passionately and stroked their cocks. But eventually Luke said that he had to get home before Emily began to wonder what was going on. Before he left, they both assured each other that sex with a man had more than lived up to each of their expectations.

In the next two weeks the guys played a lot of pool together. They tried every form of male sex they could, and loved everything and every minute of it. They had some difficulty adapting to anal sex at first, but after it was mastered, they both agreed it was the best form of man sex.

When Maureen returned, Luke began to urge Emily to take their daughter and go north to New York to escape the oppressive summer heat in Florida and possibly a hurricane or two. Luckily for Tom and Luke, she thought it was a wonderful idea.

A GAY GOTHIC TALE

My ancestral home was built many leagues from the nearest village of Rainboro, where my mother's parent's lived. The road between my home and my grandparents' home was a barely discernable dirt rut, and navigation between the two locations was difficult. The only time we made the grueling trek was at the Yuletide.

The nearest doctor was a good two hours away by swift steed. It was thus that it happened that Dr. McDrurey did not reach our house until four hours after my father died on my eighteenth birthday, which fell on the twentieth day of November. We were celebrating the event, when a small morsel of venison from my birthday meal, lodged in my father's throat. Suddenly he began to gag. We pounded on his backside, but he just kept gagging until he turned blue and collapsed. Immediately we dispatched a trusted servant to fetch the doctor, but unfortunately, it was to no avail.

We could not bury the good man for three days because we had to wait for a priest to arrive. He was laid to rest with his ancestors in the family cemetery. My mother retired to her bedroom not an hour after the internment and no amount of my cajoling could get her out of her chamber. The servants brought meals to her. They provided warm, soapy water with which she could bathe her frail body, and they regularly emptied her chamber pot. Except for the ministering of the servants, she remained alone in her room, mourning for my father.

Our home had been built centuries ago as a fortress. There were few windows and the house was dark, cold and dank even in mid summer. In all honesty, I could not blame my mother for hiding in her room. She had hated our home since the day my father brought her there after their nuptials.

When a month had passed, she allowed me to call upon her. I quickly suggested that she should visit with her parents for as long as it would please her. I had taken over the management of the farm and our estate, and if I might be allowed to brag, I was doing an excellent job of it. She resisted the idea of leaving my father's home at first, but my persistence wore her down and she consented at long last.

I outfitted a carriage for her and tied my own fine steed to the rear. I drove the carriage and accompanied my mother to my grandparents. Halfway there, I was surprised to see a rather imposing mansion about fifty yards off the rutted road. I could not remember ever having seen it before, and I made a mental note to inquire as to its inhabitants.

We arrived at my grandparents' home in Rainboro late of an afternoon. I could not linger there, and I left almost immediately, over my grandparents' objections. I explained that I needed to get home quickly as I was now overseer of the family estate, and my presence at Bradsmoor was a necessity. They embraced me and sent me on my way with a basket of food.

I was not a half hour on the road when it began to sleet. I covered my face with a great scarf that my grandmother had knitted for me years ago, and I forged ahead. My faithful steed was having much difficulty negotiating his way.

The sleet eventually turned to snow and now I could barely see before me. The white snow was blinding me and I lost all sense of direction. The road was not clearly distinguished and I began to fear for my safety. Then I saw it. There were lights ahead, warm and inviting. I realized that the lights were emanating from the house which I had not known existed prior to today.

I headed my horse toward the lights. They had appeared so close, but it seemed to take hours to get there. When I arrived at my destination, I could see a lean-to very close to the house and I tied my horse to a post in the shelter. I wiped him down with my scarf as best I could and covered him with a blanket from my saddle bag. Then I trudged my way to the front door. It was exceptionally dark and I realized that all the lights in the house, which had shone so brightly of late, were now extinguished. I prayed that if the inhabitants of this sanctuary were asleep, they would hear me banging at the door.

The knocker was heavy and ornate. It would take some strength to lift it and start knocking. To my horror and dismay, the knocker was frozen to the door and I could not budge it. I was about to start pounding on the door when it opened up.

Standing in the doorway was a handsome youth of some twenty years. He was wearing a heavily embroidered scarlet robe, and in his hand he held a candle whose flame he shielded from the wind. He beckoned me in and tight shut the front door after me. Unlike my cold house, the interior of this abode was warm and comfortable.

The youth said not a word, but motioned me to follow him. He led me into a large library. A warm fire glowed in the fireplace. The man pulled a chair close to the fire, and spoke at last.

"Take off your wet garments and hang them on the back of this chair. The fire will dry them in a very short time."

I did as he requested, and I stripped off my heavy outer coat. My waistcoat was wet as well, and I removed it also, it being quite warm in the room. Lastly I removed my wet boots and stockings.

"If your trousers or your shirt are wet, do not be shy about removing them as well," my host proclaimed. "We are the only two souls in this house, my servants having deserted me a fortnight ago."

I was perfectly dry now and not inclined to remove any more clothing, but I was after all a curious youth of eighteen. "Why have they deserted you?" I asked in all innocence.

"That is a story that would take another fortnight to relate. Just rest assured that we are alone, and that I am more than pleased to offer you my hospitality. From the looks of the falling snow, you may be here for a time. Are you hungry?" he asked.

I had devoured my grandmother's basket of food, just before stumbling on this house so I shook my head. "No thank you. I've eaten," I said.

"May I offer you a warming glass of wine then?" he asked me, sounding most hospitable.

"No thank you," I replied. "I am happily content to be out of the weather and warm and comfortable in your home. But where are my manners?" I extended my hand and said, "My name is Tom McIntyre and I live in Bradsmoor some ten miles up the road, if you can call it a road."

The handsome youth took my hand. He didn't really shake it, but he held it and I could feel warmth invade my entire body. "I am Rene LaFontaine," he said. My ancestry is French."

"It is a pleasure," I said pulling my hand away.

"Are you tired?" he asked me.

"I have to admit that fighting the elements has exhausted me."

"Let's to bed then," he said. "We'll get better acquainted in the morning." He extended his hand, which I took, and he guided me up the stairs. He opened the first door on the right at the top of the staircase.

He led us into a large bed chamber. A warm fire burned in the fireplace. The room contained a large armoire and a huge bed. I reckoned that four large men could sleep in it. I had never before seen a bed quite so large. At the foot of the bed there stood a rather heavy looking hope chest.

"Other than servants' quarters, I am afraid that this is the only bedchamber which is furnished," he said. "I must ask you to sleep with me. I promise I do not snore nor do I much toss and turn. And you?"

"I too am a quiet sleeper. Restlessness has never been a trait of my family," I assured him.

"Good," he said and dropped his robe. He faced me completely naked. He had not had on any clothing under the robe. He bent over and removed a chamber pot from under the bed and peed into it at some length. Then he offered me the pot.

"Just a moment," I said, and completely disrobed as quickly as I was able. I took the pot and did my business. He took it from me and opened the bedroom door. He placed the pot outside the door. I wondered at that, since he had no servant to dispose of our water. He closed the chamber door and secured it tightly. Again I wondered why he would take such precautions if we were alone in the house.

Now we both stood facing each other completely naked. We did what all young men do. We stared at our genitalia. I had seen my father after his bath several times. He was small and shrunken, but Rene's cock was magnificent. It was, I believe, partially erected, and at least seven inches long and quite thick. His head was pushing through his foreskin and I could see a bubble of a viscous fluid on the tip.

"Have you ever tasted a man's juices?" he asked, noting that I was staring at the bubble adorning his cock head.

"No," I replied. He took his forefinger and removed the bubble.

"Here," he said, "Taste." I was strangely titillated by all this. I had never at that time even pleasured me as yet, and I was excited and aroused at the prospect of what avenue Rene was pursuing.

I licked the fluid off his finger and was disappointed that I received no discernable taste. "It has no taste," I said.

"You'll see, I'll make more later, and it will have a pleasant taste, I assure you. Now let us get to sleep." I climbed into the bed and lay at one far end whilst Rene extinguished the candles. The room was now dimly lit only by the waning fire.

"Move closer to the center," Rene suggested, "lest ye fall off the side." As I moved closer to the center, Rene got into the bed. He pulled the covers over us and snuggled close to me. I turned away from him and he nested against me. I could feel his cock pressing against the crack of my arse. I was simultaneously frightened and aroused. My cock was now fully erected as was his.

I could feel Rene's arm encircle my waist and reach for my cock. His fingers wrapped around it and held it tight. He did not stroke it nor fondle it. He simply held it. I was petrified. After a bit, I could tell from his breathing that he had fallen asleep. As frightened as I was, I fell asleep too. The difficult journey had exhausted me.

Sometime in the middle of the night, I awoke. Rene was sleeping a little off from me and no longer wrapped around me. I had to pee again so I crept out of the bed and went out into the hallway where I knew the chamber pot to be. It was where he had left it. I bent over intending to pick it up gently so as not to spill any of our combined waste.

The pot was empty. Rene had said that we were the only souls in the house. He must have gotten out of bed and emptied it, yet I was reasonably sure he had never left our bed. I peed and left the pot outside, and returned to the bed. As soon as I got into bed, Rene wrapped himself around me again. His hand found my cock once more and encircled it. This time he began to stroke it and I had the strangest sensation.

All my fears deserted me. My cock hardened almost immediately. I felt a tingling sensation growing in my loins. It was the pleasantest tingle I had ever experienced. The tingle grew and grew in intensity. My breathing got heavy and my whole body began to writhe. Suddenly Rene stopped stroking me. He leaned over my body and took my cock in his mouth. I was awestruck. I knew it felt wondrously good, but I was unaware that my cock could be used in such a manner. I pondered the notion that he might be of the habit of ingesting urine. He continued stroking me with his tongue and the tingle returned. I began to feel like my body might turn to fire and burn itself up. A sensation of such pleasure came over me that I began to cry. I wish I could describe my first orgasm to you, but I lack the poet's talents.

I could feel some sort of emission coming from my cock and filling Rene's mouth. My cock was tender and I begged Rene to stop sucking me. He crept up my body and began to kiss me. As he did so, he passed some of my emission into my own mouth. I swallowed it and it tasted good.

"I told you I would make more fluid and you would like it," Rene told me. He turned his back to me and went to sleep. I was left with an empty feeling. I wanted to do that to him, but he had turned away from me. There was nothing for me to do but to try to sleep also.

When I awoke, the room was lighted by the dawn, but it was far from bright. The fire had been newly stoked and I felt quite warm. I was alone in the chamber. I walked to the window and peered out. The snow was still falling so heavily that I could not see beyond the window. I turned back toward the bed and I saw that the hope chest was covered with a basin of warm soapy water, a wash cloth and a towel. To my surprise the chest also contained the chamber pot. It was clean and smelled fresh washed. I needed to use the pot badly.

I placed it on the floor and squatted over it. I deposited my waste from front and rear and whilst still naked, I returned the pot to the hallway just out side the door. I used the wash cloth and the soapy water to wash my body as best I could. The last thing I did was to clean my lately discharged arse. I delicately opened the door, and dropped the now brown wash cloth atop the chamber pot.

I returned to the room and could not see my clothes. I opened the armoire and there were my garments, neatly hung. I dressed and left the room. I descended the staircase, but there seemed to be no one on the main level of the house. I followed the aroma of cooking to the next level down. There I found the kitchen. Rene was standing over a stove attending to our breakfast. He wore his trousers and a pair of slippers, and it was obvious that no under garments touched his beautiful body. He was shirtless and I longed to caress his magnificent torso. After all, he had done as much to me, but I was afraid that he was not inclined to receive my touches in a friendly manner. I feared also that I might offend him with any gesture of affection.

"Ah, there you are," Rene said. "Come here at once."

I ran up to him and he kissed me lightly on my lips. "I feared you would sleep the day away. Had you not come downstairs when you did, I would have been forced to have fetched you. Sit down at the table and I will serve you your breakfast."

I knew not what to say and so I did as he bade me. He served each of us two boiled eggs. Already sitting on the table were a fresh baked loaf of bread and a small tub of butter. I wondered where all this came from, since he was so isolated, and since he had nary a servant.

I was emboldened to ask him how the chamber pot kept getting emptied and then cleaned to be used anew as there were no servants afoot. He looked at me in a strange manner and answered me thus: "I had not noticed any such event." I knew to say no more on the matter.

"I have removed your steed from the lean-to and placed him in my stable," he informed me. "He has been combed and fed and is perfectly content as he is sharing the stable with a mare, and both are untethered."

I thanked him for being so thoughtful and so kind.

We placed all the dirty dishes and pans in a large scrub sink already filled with water, and we left them there. I could not help but wonder if phantom servants would wash the dirty dishes and return them to the cupboards.

"Come now," Rene said. "Unfortunately we have no diversions in this house and I would want to pursue the pleasures of the flesh. There is much I have yet to teach you so let's hie to the bedchamber."

There was much I was eager to learn and I hurried after him. The first thing I noticed was that the chamber pot was no longer in the hallway, but this time I swear by the virgin, I saw a running figure far down the hall, turning at the bend. I was afraid to comment at all. Rene would surely deny my sighting.

When we entered the room, the wash basin and the wet towel were gone. I knew that if I said something to Rene, he would tell me that he hadn't noticed, so I kept my tongue.

He came to me and undid the stays on my trousers and they dropped to my ankles. I stepped out of them. As I did so, my eyes naturally turned to the floor. When I looked up, Rene was already in bed and totally naked.

"Join me," he said in such a seductive manner, that I would have thought such whispers were left solely for a husband and his wife in the privacy of their bedchamber.

I jumped onto the bed and he wrapped his arms around me. He began to kiss me in a way previously unknown to me. He forced my lips apart and his tongue began to caress my own. Such caressing had so strange an affect on me, that I near swooned.

"Would you like to suck my cock," he asked "as I have so lately sucked yours?"

My body ached with a desire I had never before known. I was so weak, I could barely whisper, "Yes."

I bent over him and took his throbbing manhood into my mouth. He instructed me in the use of my tongue and lips. I must have been an excellent student, because he seemed pleased with me, and he rewarded my efforts with many sighs of pleasure. We were both so lost in our love making, that we failed to hear or notice the bedchamber door open.

Suddenly I was pulled off Rene's body and thrown on my back. I looked up to see a horribly deformed dwarf peering at me. He threw himself on my body and attempted to take my cock into his mouth. I was so revolted I thought I might give up my breakfast. I began to fight the creature, but he was so strong that I made little headway.

I felt my cock entering his mouth, and his tongue was as rough as my pet cat's. I cried out in pain. My sobs were well rewarded. In my agony I heard Rene whipping the creature across his back and buttocks.

"Off, off him, Andre," I heard Rene scream at the creature. Andre jumped off me and I was aware that he was running down the hall with Rene in close pursuit. I heard a heavy door bang shut somewhere off in the distance, and then I heard the unmistakable clang of a lock bar slide into place.

Rene returned to me weeping. I was quite in a state of shock. "He is my twin brother," Rene explained, and burst into breast racking sobs. He is the reason why we have no servants. They would hear strange noises and occasionally see strange shapes in the corridors. Believing my home to be haunted, they all departed."

That's about the moment when I fainted dead away.

When I awakened, I was in my own bed in my own home. Rene was sitting on my bed holding my hand. I glanced toward the window and was aware that the snow had stopped falling. Bright sunlight was shining into the room. I had never before noticed any brightness in my house.

Rene got up and latched my door. When he returned to me, he placed his hand on my genitals and began to rub my cock. "Would you like to continue what we started?" he asked. I nodded, and he stripped in a trice. He lay down next to me and said, "Tom, I love you."

I leaned over him and took him into me. I remembered his instructions and amidst heavy sighs, writhing of his body, and a loud scream, he spurted into me straight away. I loved the taste of him and drank every drop.

"Next time," he said, "I'll teach you how to fornicate in my arse hole."

"That will pleasure me no end," I answered him and kissed him on his lips.

"Please," I said, "tell me how I came to be home."

"After you fainted," Rene said, "I returned to Andre's room to explain that he could never commit such a dastardly act again. When I opened his door, he was lying in a pool of blood. A knife protruded from his chest. He still breathed and he whispered in my ear that he could not live like this any longer. He said he loved me, and the most precious gift he could give me was my freedom. He expired moments later and I buried him in the family crypt below the house. Nobody knows of his existence so I needn't explain his death. By my oath, I swear to you, I gave him a good Christian burial. I cleaned his room and it is free of any traces of blood.

When I returned to the bedchamber and to our shared bed, I saw that the snow had stopped. I readied my coach with two fine horses, and tied your steed to the rear of it. I dressed you and carried you into the coach. It was a difficult journey to your home, the snow being piled quite high. When I reached your front door at long last, your servants near covered me with kisses, that relieved were they to see you alive. They helped me deposit you in your own bed and allowed me to stay until you awakened."

"What are we to do now?" I asked. "Now that I have found you, I could not bear to face a life without you." I sobbed and embraced my true love.

"Our lands abut one to the other," Rene said. "Let us become one; one estate, one farm, one body. We can let our farmers live in your house, and you will live with me in mine."

The thought of living with Rene and sleeping with him every night warmed me body and soul. "Yes," I said, one body, one soul. We'll be together for eternity, here on earth, and in the life after death, still to come. I pledge myself to you, Rene."

I reached over to my night table and took hold of my letter opener. I slit the tip of my forefinger. Rene offered me his finger and I slit it likewise. We held our fingers together and mingled our blood. Then we kissed.

Author's Note: This tale is homage to the talented authors of the nineteenth century who produced all those wonderful, eerie, romantic tales. Special thanks go to the Bronte sisters. If I have offended any of them currently dwelling in paradise, I hope they will please accept my humble apologies. HB

.

BETTER THAN GOLD

Both boys were eighteen years young and they had the same dream: to win gold at the winter Olympic games. They were both speed skaters, and both had donned training skates before they could barely walk.

James Hardin was born in Montana, and Aaron Kyle was born in Colorado. Both were surrounded by great skating rinks and top notch trainers. Each began competing at the age of seven. Although they trained miles apart, they often competed against each other and that's how they met. They became good friends and looked forward to seeing each other at their meets. Nevertheless, on the ice, they each skated to win. Over the years they both scored a great number of wins, and each amassed an impressive quantity of medals.

If they weren't in the same competition, like regionals, and one of them won top honors, the other called to congratulate the winner. They would talk for hours. Their parents literally had to grab the phones away from them.

Oh yes, there was one more minor thing that they shared. It was a secret that each of them kept from the other. They knew the secret could never be revealed and never ever uttered. They were both gay and they were hopelessly in love with one another. Every night, hundreds of miles apart, they lay in their separate beds whacking off, and dreaming that they were making love to the other. Although their hearts ached, they could not allow themselves to believe that their fantasies would ever be realized.

At eighteen, they found themselves competing in the Olympic Trials. The American team could only take five speed skaters to the Olympic Games. The competitors raced in meets of differing meter lengths. James excelled in the longer races and Aaron excelled in the shorter sprints. No matter what the talents were of the five men selected, four of them at a time would race in the various relays, and one would sit it out.

For the first time the two friends were not really competing against each other. All they had to do was take first place in any one of the events and they were on the team. Aaron was rooting for James to take the long races and James was rooting for Aaron to take the shorter ones. They each desperately wanted the other to make the team so that they could go to Copenhagen together.

They did just that. When the committee announced the speed skating team, five young men stood up and shouted, but in addition, James and Aaron embraced each other in a bear hug.

They asked to be room mates in the Olympic Village and their request was granted. As soon as they unpacked, they checked the map that they had been provided with. They studied the map and located the practice rinks, the competition rinks, and most importantly, the dining room.

There was a big bulletin board at the entrance to the American dorms designed to keep the athletes aware of their responsibilities, and the assigned times for practice and training sessions. The first order of business was scheduled for 8 AM the following morning, and that was to be rehearsal for the opening ceremonies. The American flag bearer was to be Jon Sorensen, a four time medalist in skiing in former winter games.

The boys, with map in hand, headed out to find the dining room. It was time for supper. Then they intended to turn in and try to resolve their jet lag. Along the way to the dining room, they were joined by other athletes from the United States and other countries. Everyone was busy shaking hands and making introductions. The mood was friendly. Political differences were forgotten as new friendships were forged.

The menu offered a choice of chicken, meat or fish. James and Aaron both chose the chicken, only because it didn't look too different than down home chicken. While they ate, they traded jokes with each other and the other athletes. A couple of times Aaron gave James a friendly pat on the back. Although he didn't reciprocate, James liked the feel of Aaron's pats. They were more like caresses. In fact, the last time Aaron patted or caressed James on the back, their eyes met and James's eyes said, 'Gee, that felt good.' Aaron did not miss that look and said to James, "You know it's been a long day and I haven't figured out yet what time it is at home. What do you say we turn in?"

On the way to their room, they passed the showers and James said, "Let's shower tonight so we don't have to fight the crowd in the morning."

"Good thinking," Aaron answered him. In their room, they stripped and put their dirty underwear and socks in laundry bags that had been supplied to them. As much as each wanted to check the other out, they averted their eyes. They wrapped their torsos in large bath towels, and took one bar of soap with them. "We can share," James said.

They found themselves alone in the shower room. There were ten shower heads in a row, and they discreetly took a shower two or three stations apart from each other. Now they did indeed check each other out. They were both circumcised and about five inches flaccid. It was nothing to write about in the school newspaper, but at least they were about the same size. Needless to say, both had magnificent athletic bodies from all the training and workouts. James had the courage to say, "You're built like a brick shit house, man."

"You're not so bad yourself," Aaron complimented him right back.

Whether it was a conscious or a subconscious act, no one could say, but they teased each other by paying particular attention to their genital hygiene. That cleansing routine did not escape either's attention.

Aaron was struggling with his back and was tempted to ask James for an assist, but thought better of it. They dried off, wrapped themselves in the large towels and started back to their room.

When they entered the room, they locked the door. Aaron sat down on his bed and watched James put on a clean pair of boxers. "Er, I hope it won't bother you," Aaron said, "but I always sleep nude. I hate when underwear rides up on me."

James started to laugh. "I do too," he said, "but I was afraid it would bother you."

"Hell no," Aaron answered, and James threw his boxers on a chair.

They shut the light and crawled under their covers. Aaron asked, "Are you still seeing that girl you brought to our last meet before the Olympic Trials?"

James shook his head. "Nah," he said. I'm always horny, but I get more pleasure with my fist than with any girl."

"Me too," Aaron said. "A school cheerleader practically seduced me one evening, and I couldn't get it up. Then the minute I got home, I whacked off twice in a row."

James sat up in his bed. "Hey man, when was the last time you whacked off?"

"It had to be four days ago, before I left my house."

"Me too," James sighed. "You have no idea how horny I am, or maybe you do. Did you ever participate in circle jerks when you were a kid?"

"Sure I did. What were your prizes?" Aaron asked laughing.

"We had two; one for the first to cum and a second for the guy who shot the furthest." James started to laugh also, as he shared that last bit of trivia. "Hey man, let's have a circle jerk without prizes. I am so fucking horny, I'm afraid I'll cum when I put on that super tight skating outfit."

Now it was Aaron's turn to laugh. He got out of his bed and sat next to James, making sure that their thighs were touching. James did not move away from his room mate. "Let's get started, man," Aaron said. He lay back on the bed with his feet on the floor and he started to stroke his rock hard cock. James did the same and as Aaron looked over at James, he noticed that he was equally as hard.

They were only at it a minute or two, when Aaron reached over, pushed James's hand away, and started to stroke James's cock. "I'm sorry," he said. "I couldn't resist."

"It's OK," James whispered. "Let me do the same for you."

As they were stroking each other, they began to moan softly and to breathe harder. Both felt their orgasms approaching and as they did, they turned toward one another and began kissing. The kisses became more and more passionate as their orgasms went beyond stopping. As they came, their tongues dueled, and they almost gagged on each other's saliva.

Most of their cum had landed on their chests, and they both started licking up as much of the other's cum as they could. They collapsed on James' bed, and resumed kissing each other.

"I have wanted to do that with you, forever," Aaron confessed. "It is always you I dream of when I whack off."

"Me too!" James said.

"James, I'm gay. I've known it for years now, and I've also known that I love you."

"Me too," was all James could manage to say again, in utterly happy amazement.

They went to sleep in one bed, wrapped up so tightly, it's a wonder they could breathe.

"When did you first know you were gay, and when did you first know that you loved me?" Aaron asked James while pressing his cock harder against him.

"Do you remember that meet in Dayton when we were about thirteen? I won the 500 meter and you won the 100 meter. My race was after yours and you came over to congratulate me. But instead of shaking my hand you gave me a great big hug. Your rock hard cock rubbed against mine, and right then and there I knew a lot of things. First off, I think that's when I realized that I was gay. Second, I knew then that I was definitely in love with you, and third, that's when I decided that I was going to spend the rest of my life with you. When did you first become aware that you were gay?"

"At least a year or two before that, but I think I loved you before I ever realized that I was gay. God, we have wasted so much time." With that they began to fall asleep, fondling each other's cocks and tickling each other's ass holes. Just as he lost consciousness, Aaron was certain that he heard James whisper, "There is so much more I want to do with you. I don't want to leave any part of your body untouched and unexplored." Smiling, Aaron fell asleep.

The rehearsal lasted until lunch time. There really wasn't much to do. All they had to do was to march in after the flag bearer and wend their way to their assigned seats in the stadium. One of the producers showed them where to go. There would be no rehearsal for the closing ceremonies. By then the competitions were over. The athletes would enter the arena randomly and sit wherever they pleased in the area designated for them.

After lunch, the real test began. They reported to the practice rinks. Before actually skating, their coach put them through some very rigorous exercises, and then ordered them to the ice.

James and Aaron warmed up side by side. They kept looking at each other and smiling. They were so obviously in a goofy mood, that the coach was prompted to ask, "What are you two ass holes grinning at? This is serious business."

"We're just happy to be here and to have made it this far," James lied for both of them.

As was expected, both boys made all the cuts in all the heats for all the races they were entered in. In speed skating the skaters don't skate in a pack. It's not a question of who comes in first, but who has the fastest time. The skaters skate two at a time, crossing each other's lanes at designated intervals to assure equality throughout the race.

The first final was a 500 meter race. Both boys were entered in this competition. Aaron skated first against a Canadian. He started out like greased lightening, but unfortunately, he began to sag after about 300 meters. Still he made excellent time. James skated against a Russian and he didn't get really lubed up until after 250 meters. In the last fifty meters he emulated Aaron's streak of lightening, and he skated fast enough to take silver, and Aaron took the bronze. They hugged each other unashamedly on the award podium and then shook hands with the Russian gold medalist.

Their next final for the Americans was a 1000 meter relay, which was scheduled in the late afternoon of the same day. Since each man had to race 250 meters, the coach had Aaron sit this one out. The American team took the gold. That ended the first day of competition.

Both boys were starved and ordered steaks that evening in the dining room. They were invited to join some of the others who were going out on the town that evening. James declined, citing that he was racing the 1500 meters individual early the next day. Aaron said that he was skating the 100 meters afterwards. Actually, they couldn't wait to get to their room.

Again they showered in the evening, and again the shower room was empty. This time they showered next to each other and copped a grab now and then. They helped each other wash their backs and had an opportunity to scrub each other's balls and ass holes. More of their fantasies were coming true.

Back in their room, James threw himself on top of Aaron's naked body. The two friends kissed as their tongues flicked across each other sensuously. James began to work his way down Aaron's body. With each kiss Aaron moaned louder. First, James kissed Aaron's neck and then he worked down to his nipples. He tweaked Aaron's nipples with his tongue and his finger tips and Aaron's moans grew louder.

He made it a point to avoid Aaron's cock, but he kissed his balls and flicked his tongue across Aaron's crack. He worked his way down both of Aaron's muscular thighs and legs. He sucked on every one of Aaron's toes. Aaron's moans were becoming little screams. Finally he cried, "You're torturing me. Please stop."

James then went right to his target. He enveloped Aaron's cock with the palm of his hand and started stroking gently. Then he kissed Aaron's engorged head very tentatively, gobbling up the precum. He stopped to say, "Oh honey, you taste so good." Then he took Aaron full in his mouth. His tongue slithered up and down the shaft and across the head. Aaron's whole body was gyrating and he looked like he was in great pain. In fact, he was writhing in uncontrollable ecstasy. "Don't stop," he pleaded. "I love you. I love you so much."

His warm sweet juices spurted into James's mouth and down his throat. When he came up for air, James pulled himself up and kissed Aaron, offering him some of his own cum.

After Aaron recovered, he said to James, "You are so fucking good. You've done this before, haven't you?"

"No, I swear. You are my first and you are going to be my only." The boys kissed harder and more passionately.

Then Aaron asked James, "would you like a blow job or would you like to fuck me?'

James was quick to answer. "I've never had either. Let's stick to oral tonight and tomorrow we can corn hole each other." Then he added, "If that's OK with you, that is."

"You're a real jerk dude," Aaron chided. "Whatever you want is OK with me." With that said, he lowered his mouth on to James's waiting cock.

On the following day, James was scheduled to race his longest race of the games. He and one other of his American team mates had made the cut to the finals. Aaron was not scheduled to skate the 100 until later that afternoon so he was in the stands saying little prayers for both Americans, but especially for James.

James skated first against a Japanese. As usual, he started slowly, conserving his energy, and after the first lap he was several meters behind. When he felt fully warmed up he made his move. Slowly lap by lap he began to close the gap on his opponent. With one lap to go, suddenly James opened up. He put on a burst of speed that shocked the crowd. He left his opponent far behind, and finished the race at least five meters ahead of the Japanese.

When all the races for the 1000 meter were concluded, James took the gold and the other American took the silver. James still had two more individual races and three relays yet to skate. With two gold medals and a silver already under his belt, James was well on the way to becoming an Olympic hero, if not a legend.

Aaron couldn't wait to get to the locker room to congratulate James. On the way, he saw that James and the silver medalist were being interviewed by a CNN reporter. He waited until the interview was over and joined them on the way to the locker room. Walking side by side with James, he put his arm around James's shoulder, and he whispered in his ear, "This is how it will always be. You and I will walk side by side forever." James turned toward him and he had a tear in his eye.

"In case you didn't figure it out yet, I'm skating to win to make you proud of me," James told Aaron.

Before they were aware of it, James and his team mate were being hustled to the podium to receive their medals. It was hard to say who was happier, James or Aaron.

Later that afternoon it was James's turn to sit in the stands and silently pray for Aaron and two other Americans who had qualified for this meet. The 100 meters is a fast and furious meet. It is over almost as soon as it begins. You need strength for a very short distance so you can go all out and let yourself go. There is no need to conserve energy, and no holding back. That makes it an exiting race and a trying one. Many spectators believe that the longer races tax the athletes and test their endurance more than shorter races, but the short sprints are probably even more grueling.

Aaron was skating against a Swede. He had a magnificent start. He looked like a thoroughbred horse coming out of the gate to run one of the triple crowns. He took the lead quickly and never lost it. When it was all over, Aaron took gold and one of the other Americans took bronze. Aaron broke an Olympic record, and he knew how he and James would celebrate this evening. That would be better than any record or any medal.

That night in their room, James reached into his airline carry on bag and retrieved a tube of KY jelly. He showed it to Aaron and said, "I brought it just in case. You see, I was hoping."

Aaron was pleased but a little embarrassed, and he began to blush. James sat down next to him, and said, "You don't have to do this if you don't want to, but I sure want you to fuck me."

"Of course, I want to, but it's all so new, you've got to cut me some slack. Anyway, I have been reading a lot of male porn on the internet, and I think I know how to get us ready. Roll onto your stomach," he instructed. Aaron took the tube and squirted some lube on James's ass hole. He used one finger to spread the jelly inside. After greasing James, he asked how it felt.

"Keep that finger moving around in there. It feels great."

Encouraged, Aaron started to insert another finger, but withdrew it quickly. He added more jelly and reinserted it easily. James said, "It hurt at first, but now it feels wonderful. Let's try the real thing."

"OK. Get on all fours," Aaron instructed. Then he lubed his cock and positioned the head at James's hole. "The porn stories always say that you should push out like you are shitting," Aaron explained. James did as he was told and Aaron began his descent. He had greased James really well, and to his surprise he went in easily. He pushed slowly until he was all the way in. James was moaning loudly, but Aaron didn't know if it was pain or pleasure. He was afraid to move and just lay there, doggie fashion, not sure what to do next.

"Tell me what to do," he pleaded with James.

"Aaron, I can't describe how good you feel inside of me. Just start humping slowly and speed up if I tell you to. When the time comes, empty inside of me." With much trepidation Aaron started humping. He couldn't believe how hot and wet James's ass was. He knew he wouldn't last long. He wanted to prolong his pleasure, but he also knew that the sooner he was done, the sooner he would get to feel James inside of him.

Aaron increased his strokes in length and intensity. Before he could even warn James, he came with such ferocity that he wailed like a banshee and then tried to muffle the sound to no avail. He stayed inside of James as long as possible and James was sad to feel him leave. All the time he was inside of James, he kissed him on the back of his neck, where James was a wee bit ticklish. When he was out of James, he rolled over on his back and James did the same.

"That was awesome. You're going to love it," James told Aaron. But I want to fuck you on your back so I can see your face, and kiss you when I cum."

Aaron was already on his back, so James placed a pillow under his buttocks and inserted first one, and then two lubricated fingers into Aaron's ass. He worked them around trying to stretch his lover out. For his part, Aaron was already lifting his body in anticipation of what was to come. James lubed his cock and placed it in striking position. He went in almost as easily as Aaron had. He figured that he and Aaron were predestined to be lovers, given how easily they were able to enter each other. Neither had experience enough to know, but they would find out that this position produced more intense orgasms, at least for them, because they could see their lover's eyes.

After James came, they embraced each other, trying to lie as close together as possible. James whispered in Aaron's ear, "The next time I'm going to lubricate you with my tongue." Aaron smiled and eventually they slept.

Both of them skated in the remaining three relays. Aaron was always the first to skate. Because of his short distance speed, he was able to get the team off to a good start. James skated last because he knew best how to close out a race. The Americans took two gold medals and a silver. James earned two more gold medals for his remaining two individual races, setting new world records in both.

There were four days left until closing ceremonies and the American speed skating team was finished with competition. Aaron and James used the time to shop and see the sights of Copenhagen. American reporters would not leave the medalists alone, hounding them wherever they went, and treating them like the heroes they were.

As the time to go home approached, they grew more and more morose. They would no longer be in competition and they lived hundreds of miles apart. The thought of being separated weighed heavily upon both of them.

They were both in their senior year in high school and Aaron got an idea. "Let's apply to the same college," he said at breakfast on their last day. "There's not a school in the country that would turn away two Olympic multi-medalists. After we graduate we can get jobs in the same city and live together happily ever after as the story books say. Perhaps we can buy an ice skating rink where we can train young athletes, but also open it to the public for recreational use."

"Great idea," James said. "We are going to have plenty of money to open a rink from all the endorsements we have both been promised. Where should we apply to go to college?"

"Let's go far away, like UCLA or USC. I've heard that LA is very gay friendly."

"Done," James agreed. They sealed their pact with a high five.

That night they made love for what would be the last time for nearly six months, until they entered their dorm room at UCLA. Afterward, lying next to each other, totally exhausted, James reflected on the events of the last two weeks.

"You know," he said stroking Aaron's cheek, "finding out how much in love we were with each other, and committing to be together for a life time, means a hell of a lot more to me than all the gold, silver or bronze in Copenhagen."

"I agree," Aaron said. They embraced and kissed each other tenderly as sleep overcame them.

LET'S PLAY

Time: Just before dawn. The present.

Place: The master bedroom of an upscale apartment on the
        upper west side of Manhattan

ACT ONE
SCENE ONE

The furniture is expensive but sparse. A king size bed sits stage right. There is a bed stand with a lamp on each side of the bed. Next to the bed stand, stage front and right, there is a closed door leading to a walk in closet. On stage left an armoire and dresser stand side by side. Next to the armoire a closed door leads to a hallway. Next to the dresser an open door leads to the master bathroom. The bathroom door is open and a sink and commode are clearly visible. A large picture window occupies stage rear. The window is covered by sheer curtains but a hint of the Manhattan skyline is visible.

As the curtain rises two men covered by a bed sheet are lying on opposite sides of the bed. The room is dimly lit, but lightens gradually as the sun rises. One of the men is snoring quite loudly. Suddenly the other one sits up and socks the snorer on his arm. The snoring stops, but the man continues to sleep.

The man who sat up is now seen naked from his waist up. The bed sheet continues to shield his lower body. Sleepily he gets out of bed. He has a beautiful, muscular body. As he stands, he stretches his arms and then adjusts his penis in the bikini underwear he is wearing. He walks to the bathroom and he can be seen peeing with his back to the audience.

While he is peeing, the other person resumes snoring. His snoring gets louder and louder. His bed mate gets back in bed and socks him again. The snoring stops.

Joe: (*yelling*) Screw you Richie. Are you ever going to stop snoring and let me get some sleep?

Richie: (*sitting up with his eyes closed*) Whaaa?

Joe: (*softening his tone*) Please Richie, stop snoring. I need to sleep.

Richie wiggles up to Joe and snuggles against him. He throws an arm across Joe's chest.

Richie: I got plenty of sleep last night. What the fuck time did you get home?

Joe: About an hour ago, I think.

Richie: Great! And what bimbo Twinkie did you screw last night? Or was it you who got screwed?

Joe: Hey, just don't start that shit with me again. You know damn well that when I said that I would move in with you, we had an agreement. We agreed that we didn't have to be monogamous.

Richie: You're right. I don't give a shit who you sleep with as long as you're careful. All I ask is that when you aren't coming home, would you please call me. Is that too much to ask? I waited up for you until midnight. Dammit, Joe, I could have been having some fun too.

Joe: Calling home like a high school teenager was not part of the agreement. Look, let me get some sleep and we'll talk later.

Richie: You're a fuck Joe, Yeah, we'll talk later.

Blackout. The stage darkens for a few seconds. When the lights go on again, the room is bright with late morning sunshine. Joe is alone in bed. The door to the hallway is open. After a second or two, Richie enters through the open door. He is bare-footed and bare-chested, but he is wearing a pair of gym shorts. He walks over to Joe to see if he is still sleeping, and then he shakes Joe's shoulder.

Richie: It's almost noon Joe. Are you going to sleep forever?

Joe does not budge. Richie turns to leave when suddenly Joe's arm shoots out and grabs Richie pulling him into bed with him. He embraces Richie and begins to kiss him. At first Richie resists but finally responds by kissing Joe back.

Joe: Jerk! Don't you know how much I love you? If I've told you once, I've told you a million times. Love is a commitment. I'm totally committed to you, but sex is for fun. I need to have fun with different guys. I can't seem to help it. I know it irks you, but I can't change.

Richie: I know. I try to be adult and urbane about it. God knows the last thing I want to impose upon us are middle class, heterosexual values about the sanctity of marriage, but I get jealous. I don't want to share you. The least you can do is bring the guy home and we can have him together.

Joe: (*pulling Richie closer to him*) Bullshit! I know you would never want to do that.

Richie: (*kissing Joe on his forehead*) You're right of course. But Joey, I'm so scared. I'm so scared of losing you.

Joe: (*kissing Richie on his lips*) It ain't gonna happen, Babe. I love you and only you.

Richie: Show me.

Richie covers the both of them with the bed sheet. He reaches under the bed sheet and it is clear that he is removing his gym shorts and briefs. He throws them on the floor. Joe does the same with his briefs. The two men wrap their arms around each other.

Joe: Let's make it quick. I'm starving.

Richie: You total prick!

Richie sits up on the edge of the bed and retrieves his underwear and shorts. He puts them on. The audience can see enough of him to be teased and titillated.

Richie: Get your ass into the kitchen I'll rustle you up some grub.

He exits. The stage darkens for a few minutes.

ACT ONE
SCENE TWO

The room is now lit only by moonlight. It is night. Off stage a door has opened and closed, but no voices are heard. Joe enters the bedroom and flicks a switch. The two bedside lamps illuminate. Joe sits on the bed and begins to remove his sneakers and socks. Richie enters sullenly.

Joe: Are you going to be pissed at me all night?

Richie: Probably.

Joe: What now?

Richie: You know very well what. You totally ignored me all evening. You danced all night with that bimbo and your fucking hand never left his crotch.

Joe: For God's sake Richie. I was only having fun. The twink was so scared, he didn't even get hard. I think it was the first time he was ever in a gay bar. Besides, I came home with you, didn't I? I wish you could leave the green eyed monster out in the lobby somewhere. How many times do I have to tell you? It's you I love.

As he speaks Joe has stripped naked. His back is to the audience and he climbs into bed covering himself quickly. Richie has remained silent as he begins to strip also. When he is naked, he shuts the lights and he gets into bed on the other side. The audience is teased a little more with quick glimpses of his genitalia.

Richie: I know that I shouldn't be jealous, but just like you can't resist the twinkies, I can't help being jealous.

The lovers snuggle up to each other. They rub their bodies together and begin to kiss. Their activity is barely visible in the moonlight, but there is no question that they have begun to make passionate love.

Joe: You're a major fool Richie. I couldn't live without you, even if I do want a Twinkie now and then.

Richie: You call two or three times a week, now and then?

Joe: Please shut up. Let me show you how much I love you.

He kisses Richie and slithers under the bed sheet. Suddenly Richie's body bucks and he begins to sigh and moan. His moans grow louder and stronger as the bed sheet bobs up and down. Finally Richie screams loudly. The head under the bed sheet stops bobbing and Joe re-emerges. He leans over Richie and kisses him passionately.

Joe: Does that tell you something?

Richie: (*kissing Joe*) Yes, it does. It tells me that I want to do the same thing to you.

Joe: Not until you promise me that you truly believe that you are the only one I love, and that any dalliance I may have with a twinkie is pure recreational sex, maybe even lust. It does not diminish how much I love you. Please say you understand and get off my back.

Richie: I'll try to understand, but now, my love, it's time for you to get on your back.

The two men lean into each other and kiss as the stage slowly darkens.

When the curtain fell at the end of the first act the two actors rushed to the dressing room they shared. They were totally naked. As soon as they closed their door they embraced, kissed and fondled their cocks.

"You shithead," Mark said. Zack began to laugh his head off.

Mark and Zack had met at the auditions for the play. There was an instant chemistry between them. It was obvious to the casting director, as well as everyone else, that they made a great couple. They were given the roles of the two characters in this two character play.

All during rehearsal, Zack who was playing Joe kept threatening Mark that he would give him a real blow job under the bed sheet on opening night. Mark told him that he better not, but Zack said that he wanted to see how professional Mark would be under the circumstances.

"Shithead," Mark said and then repeated. "Shithead, you really did it."

"Yes, and you were able to complete the scene. My dick is doffed to you. You were very professional. I'd ask for equal treatment, but we have to get dressed for Act Two."

In the second act both actors are fully dressed. The act takes place in the living room of their apartment. Richie's jealously has finally taken all it can take, and the two lovers are splitting. They argue over what belongs to whom, and as they argue they recall the special circumstance they shared when they bought the object they are arguing over. Little by little they realize how bound up together their lives have become. Slowly they realize that they can't live apart and the act ends as they strip naked, and enter the door to the bedroom. The living room is empty as the stage darkens.

Zack and Mark put robes on for their curtain call, but some of the audience yells for them to drop the robes. They smile at each other, holding hands and bow to the applause.

Back in their dressing room, they remove their makeup and get into their street clothes.

"Are you going to blow me again every night?" Mark wants to know.

"Nope," Zack answers. "You know what they say in the theater. Always leave them wanting more."

Outside the theater they go their separate ways.

During the course of rehearsals, they had become good friends and they had made it together a couple of times, but neither had realized that they had fallen in love. So on this very successful opening night, they didn't even think to celebrate together.

Mark knew of a rather quiet gay bar on East 86th Street called Dudes. It was a more intimate spot than most other bars in the city. He had arranged to meet some friends there after the performance whether the play was a success or not. He could only hope the critics loved it as much as the predominantly gay opening night audience seemed to have.

He wasn't there more than five minute sipping his first gin and tonic when he spotted Zack coming in to the bar. Zack was greeted by a few well wishers when he spotted Mark. He immediately went over to Mark and kissed him on the lips.

"Gee, I'm glad you're here," Zack said. "We should have agreed to celebrate together in the first place."

A strange thing happened that night. No matter how many friends tried to get their attention, Mark and Zack remained glued to each other. They had no idea that there were other people in the bar. They were in a world of their own. They had fallen hopelessly in love before this night, but now they were finally aware of it.

Suddenly Mark started to giggle like a school girl.

"What?" Zack asked.

"Let's switch parts tomorrow. I know all your lines and you know mine. Then I can give you an onstage blow job at the end of Act One. In fact, I think it would be fun to alternate roles so neither of us gets stale. It's been done before especially in two character plays."

Zack looked seriously at Mark. "It's a wonderful idea he said, "but I don't think I can wait until tomorrow night for you to go down on me. Please spend the night with me." He took Mark's hand and they left the bar. Their friends were still celebrating and nobody even noticed when they left.

So far neither of them had said the magic words, but as they walked hand and hand to Zack's nearby apartment, Mark leaned over and whispered in Zack's ear, "I love you Zack."

"I love you more," Zack said and squeezed Mark's hand even tighter. When they got home Mark gave Zack what he couldn't wait for and a whole lot more.

At the theater the next night, they told the director about their idea for alternating their roles. The director wasn't sure, but he said that they could do it that evening and he would decide after the performance.

As Act One, Scene Two drew to an end, it was Mark's turn to go down on Zack. The scene was played much differently than the night before. Mark had moaned and groaned with pleasure but Zack was so amused by the whole idea that he kept giggling. The audience believed that he was acting as if he was very ticklish and they laughed along with him. As his passion grew, however, he began to moan and sigh just like Mark had the night before. The audience felt his segue from fun to passion in their own groins, and somehow, as well as Mark had played it (it was real after all), Zack's unintended interpretation was something the audience had no trouble relating to.

When the curtain fell, the director told them, that they could indeed alternate the two roles, but he asked Mark to put a little comedy in the blow job scene just as Zack had. The two lovers broke into gales of laughter, but declined to explain their amusement to the director.

Mark's tenancy was month to month, and he moved in with Zack as soon as proper notice was given. The nightly audiences could not get over how convincing their love scenes were.

One day when the theater was dark, Zack brought home a young twinkie whose territory was Eighth Avenue in midtown Manhattan. It was just intended as a joke and to tease Mark. The twinkie and they fully expected to have a three way, but at the end of the day, neither Mark nor Zack could do it. They wined and dined the young man, paid him and sent him on his way.

Alone together that night Mark kissed Zack delicately on the lips and said, "You are all I need or ever will."

Zack returned the delicate kiss and said, "Ditto."

Art does not always imitate life or vice versa.

TEACHER! TEACHER!

I got my first job two weeks before graduating college. I secured a position teaching fifth grade in an elementary school on the upper east side of Manhattan in the Yorkville section of town. There was nothing special about me, then or now. I was average height, average build, and thinning hair at twenty-three, average size circumcised cock, average amount of sexual encounters per week (maybe once a month). You might say my only outstanding feature was my love of teaching and my love and faith in children.

Not too far from the school, there was a very intimate bar tucked away between two German restaurants. Yorkville is basically a neighborhood of people of German descent. The front of the bar was very unpromising as a place to spend an enjoyable evening. It was certainly no 'Cheers.' It consisted of one average size door. Over the door there hung a rather small sign that read 'Dudes'. From the appearance of the frontage, you would think that the whole interior of the bar was the width of the door. Well that's near the truth. Once inside, the bar stretched about six feet on each side of the door. The whole place was about fifteen feet wide, but about forty feet deep.

The clientele of the bar were mainly young to middle age men who worked in the area. Rowdy young twinkies went elsewhere to dance and make out. Dudes was a pretty staid place for a gay bar, so staid that its existence never impacted on the two surrounding restaurants. It turned out that the owner of one of the restaurants was of a mind to frequent the bar himself.

I lived within walking distance of the school and therefore within walking distance of the bar. Two or three times a week after I consumed a meager and lonely bachelor dinner at home, I would walk over to the bar. I got friendly with a few of the other regulars and I even scored there once in a while, but that was not my main purpose to be there. It was where I went to spend a few friendly hours a week, away from my solitude.

In the middle of January, in my second year at the school, I went to bed one evening and started to sneeze, and then I started to cough. I didn't sleep at all that night. My throat was rough and sore and I couldn't talk or swallow. My temperature reached 103 degrees. Hot tea with honey did not relieve me at all. For the first time ever, I called in sick and ran to my doctor. He told me that I had the Asian flu, prescribed some medication, advised bed rest, and finally admonished me to drink plenty of fluids.

This particular school year there had been no openings for new teachers in our school. The graduating class after mine was having a tough time finding employment. School budgets had been cut drastically and raises had been minimal for those of us who were happily employed. Notwithstanding all this, the school administration had put two graduates on the roster as substitutes with the promise of regular employment as the openings occurred. I am happy to say that both these fine teachers were regulars by the next school year. One of them was a woman, Janet Blake, and the other was a young man, Robert Bondie. Robbie took over my class.

I returned almost ten school days later and was astonished to find that my class was right up to snuff. Substitute teachers never get respect from their classes, which makes learning (and teaching) difficult. It seemed to me that Mr. Bondie had done a great job. My students were ecstatic. They were ebullient in informing me of how much they liked him and what a great teacher he was. Needless to say that made me a little shaky, until one sweet little girl told me that I was a great teacher also.

At lunch time, I went to the office and found out that Robbie was teaching another class and was in the school. I was determined to meet this master teacher, so the minute the school bell announced the end of the day, I ran over to the class room where he was teaching. I got there just as he was packing a small back pack in preparation of his departure.

I walked in and stuck out my hand. "Hi," I said, "I'm John Corbin. You taught my class for the past couple of weeks."

"Oh yes," he said, "It's a pleasure to meet you." He extended his hand and I took it. I don't know how I got through the next few seconds. When Robbie took my hand, electric bolts went through my body, and I know I held on way too long, but I just couldn't let go. As average a guy as I was, he was leagues beyond me. He was about six feet tall. Even below his winter attire, I could see his ripped body. His hair was straight and ebony black and his eyes were ice blue. He was so handsome, I nearly swooned.

"The kids were telling me how much they liked you and what a good teacher you are and I just had to meet Mr. Wonderful," I managed to stammer out.

Robbie started to laugh. "You can relax," he said. "They said the same thing about you." Then we both laughed.

"Well," I said, "I'll see you around."

Robbie taught almost constantly that year. It seemed that the flu and other ailments were rampant among the teaching staff. We ran into each other in the hallways often, and occasionally had lunch together in the teacher's lounge. But that was the extent of our relationship. Robbie kept talking about his girl friend and then he started talking about their upcoming wedding. He was straight, and as attracted to him as I was, there was nothing I could do about it.

Towards the end of that year, one of the young female teachers handed in her resignation effective with the end of the school year. She was getting married and moving to Seattle. Janet got her job. Robbie and I were both disappointed for one day. Then another older teacher resigned because her husband was being transferred to Phoenix. Tada! Robbie would now be a regular next school year.

As the year drew to a close, I asked Robbie one day when he was getting married and what he was doing this summer.

"I was going to go back to my home in Trenton," he said. There's a community center there that offered me a job coaching basketball in their summer programs, but I'm not going to do it. I think I'll take some summer courses here in New York instead." As he said that he looked down and sounded very sad.

"What's wrong?" I asked. "I can tell something's wrong."

"My engagement is off," he stated simply.

My heart began to beat a little faster and I know that my blood pressure rose, but what could I do? Nothing! I wanted to comfort him and offer to take him out to dinner or something, but I was so afraid of my own emotions that I remained silent. If I made a move on a straight man, he would either shrug it off or slug me. I didn't want to risk his friendship.

"Buck up," I said I'll see you tomorrow.

"I'm bucked up," he said. "I'm the one who broke it off." He turned and left me gaping after him.

As it turned out I never did see him again before school ended. The regular teachers stayed healthy and they all finished off the year. In fact, the summer was nearly over and I still hadn't seen Robbie. I wanted to call him often but resisted the urge. I could have called to see how he was doing, but since he told me that he had been the one to break the engagement, there didn't seem to be much reason to check on him.

It was mid August. I hadn't had much luck in the romance department lately, and I was feeling sorry for myself. It was one of those Saturday evenings that saw no respite from the heat of the dog day afternoon. The air was hot, sultry, and very humid. I decided to walk over to Dudes for a cool one. By the time I got there my tank top was ringing wet.

I was surprised to find the place nearly deserted, but I shouldn't have been. Dudes' main business was after work at happy hour. I sat down at the bar and asked for a cold, very cold, Bud Light. After I took my first sip of the refreshing beverage, I looked around to see if I knew anyone there. My eyes finally hit on the far end of the bar. Someone was sitting there all alone, holding a beer bottle and looking very, very unhappy. I recognized him immediately. It was Robbie.

My heart started beating faster than a speeding bullet. I was in a panic and I wanted to run, but my ass was glued to my bar stool. Robbie was looking down and I knew he could not see me. That gave me some time to think.

Robbie had told me that he broke the engagement. Did he do that because he was gay? He had to be gay if he was in Dudes, or did he just wander in here by accident, not realizing that the bar was for men only? My heart beat began to slow down, and I began to think a little more clearly.

If Robbie had wandered in here by mistake and didn't know the place was gay, he still wouldn't know I was gay if I went over to him. On the other hand, if he was gay, and he knew exactly where he was, I didn't mind in the least outing myself to him. My decision was made. I decided that I was definitely going to go over and ask how he was doing. Obviously he wasn't doing well based upon his demeanor.

I picked up my beer bottle and ambled down to the end of the bar. I came up behind him and put my arm around his shoulder.

"Robbie, my friend," I said. "What's wrong? You look like you were just hit by a truck." He looked up to see who was being so intimate with him. When he saw who it was, his sad, sad face broke out into a big grin.

"Johnny," he said, half laughing, half sobbing. "I so need a friend right now." I was still holding his shoulder but he jumped up and threw his arms around me, hugging me hard. He turned around and spied an empty table in a far corner. He motioned toward the table and we went over to it and sat down.

"First of all," he began, "what the fuck are you doing in a gay bar? I would have bet a bundle that you were straight."

"I would have bet two bundles that you were the straight one," I countered. He smiled at me and took one of my hands in both of his. Then he began his narrative.

"I had gone home to Trenton the weekend before I told you that my wedding was off. I tried hard to go through with it, but I knew I couldn't lie any longer to myself or to anyone who knew me. I came out to my fiancée and to my parents. She slapped my face, called me a bastard, and ran off somewhere. My parents disowned me and told me they never wanted to see me again. I'm not sad about what I did, or about my fiancée calling me a bastard, but I am sad and disappointed at my parents' reaction. I would have hoped for more love and understanding."

I laid my free hand on top of his. "Now it's my turn to confess," I said. From the first moment that we shook hands, I've had strong feelings for you. I thought you were straight and I suppressed those feelings. Now I can be truthful and tell you that I would like to pursue a relationship with you."

"What jerks we were to waste all this time," Robbie said. "I've pretty much felt the same way. In fact it was my feelings for you that prompted me to be honest with myself and to come out."

"Why the hell didn't you call me?" I asked.

"I thought you were straight, and I didn't want to spoil our friendship, such as it was," he answered.

"I didn't call you for the same reason," I said. Then I leaned forward across the tiny table and I kissed Robbie. It was a very chaste kiss and lasted only a second but those electric bolts invaded my body once again.

"You should know that I am a virgin as far as man sex is concerned," Robbie confessed. "I did sleep with my girlfriend a couple of times, but it didn't send me to Nirvana."

"I'd like a chance to do that for you. Would you like me to send you to Nirvana?" I asked Robbie as I squeezed his hand tightly. He didn't say anything but he nodded his head. We sat silently for awhile, staring at each other and smiling.

Finally he said, "I've got a pretty solid hardon, and I'd hate to have to do something about it by myself."

I stood up so he could see my tenting gym shorts. "I live really close by. I'd love for you to come home with me." He smiled broadly at me, and we got up to leave. I held his hand all the way home, not caring who saw us.

The moment we got into my apartment and locked the door, we started kissing wildly. There was nothing chaste about our kisses now. Our tongues locked in a duel and we started to pull off our skimpy clothing. It didn't take long for us to stand facing each other naked. Robbie's circumcised cock was at least an inch and a half bigger than mine, but he stared at my hard cock as if it was the most beautiful thing he had ever seen.

"Can I touch it?" he asked me. His voice was shaking.

"If you don't I'll go crazy," I answered him. As I said that, I wrapped my palm around his cock and started to stroke it gently. He did the same to me. I led him into the bedroom and we threw ourselves on the bed still kissing.

"Lie on your back," I commanded. Robbie turned over and I began to move down his body, lingering in all the right places. I took little bites out of his neck. He was going to have a very purple hickey in the morning. Then I went down to his nipples, sucking, kissing and nipping at them. By this time Robbie was moaning and writhing in pleasure.

I sucked hard on his innie, trying to vacuum it out, and then I went down to his abdomen. I buried my tongue in his untrimmed pubes and heard him making little whining sounds. I carefully avoided his throbbing cock, being sure not to touch it. I started to suck on his balls and then the inside of his thighs. I worked down to his ankles and then sucked on all ten of his toes, giving each equal attention. By now he was lifting his body off the bed and I thought he might be crying so I decided to end his agony. I leaned on my knees between his legs and took his cock into my mouth. I always sucked cock from this angle so that my tongue could slide up and down the underside of my partner's shaft. That's where I knew I was giving him the most pleasure.

Robbie's moans grew louder and then, with a wailing shriek, he came. I was glad my A/C was on and the windows were closed. His shriek was so loud, I bet his parents could hear him in Trenton. I tried to swallow all of his sweet juices, but he shot out a gallon and some of it began to dribble from my mouth.

I scooted up his body and placed my mouth on his. To my astonishment and my delight, he began to suck in and swallow his own cum.

I rolled over on my side, making sure that our bodies were touching. Everything was silent. Neither of us said a word and then I heard Robbie crying like a baby. "That was so wonderful," he sobbed. "I knew it would be great, but I never knew how great. Thank you Johnny, thank you."

We lay there without moving. We both needed recovery time from our recent encounter. Of course, I needed relief, and I had an erection so stiff, it hurt. What surprised me was that Robbie never lost his erection and he was twitching like he was raring to go again.

Suddenly he rolled over and took my cock in his mouth. He tongued the head and all around the shaft. He stopped sucking for a moment and said to me, "It tastes better than I had ever imagined," and he went back to sucking me. I could tell he was trying to emulate me, but he was very inept.

"Get between my legs and take it so that your tongue is on the underside of my cock. Use your tongue more than your lips and try to keep your teeth out of the picture," I instructed him. "My erogenous zone is the underside of my cock."

What a quick learner my lover was. He did as I instructed and he brought me to ecstasy in short order. He also swallowed most of my cum and then offered the rest to me. I took it eagerly, and as I did so our tongues resumed their dueling battle of love. After several minutes we lay still together getting our strength back.

"Johnny!" Robbie said. "It was Nirvana." I smiled, rolled on top of him, and we resumed kissing as our still erect cocks ground together. Robbie had his arms wrapped so tightly around me that I could hardly breathe.

"How soon will you teach me how to fuck?" he asked me.

"Soon, my love, soon," I answered. I wrapped my arms around Robbie, making sure that our cocks were touching and that's how we fell asleep.

The morning came hot and sunny. I jumped out of bed and pulled down the shades to keep the room as dark as possible. Robbie was still asleep and snoring ever so lightly. It was more like heavy breathing. I feasted my eyes on his magnificent athletic body and tears began to well up. I went into the bathroom to relieve myself and I brushed my teeth.

When I went back to the bedroom, Robbie was sitting up and smiling at me. "I need a shower," he said to me as he bounded out of bed to pee.

"So do I," I said. "Do you mind if I ask you to brush your teeth. I have designs on your mouth." I didn't have a new toothbrush so I offered him my own saying, "If you can suck my cock you can use my tooth brush." That must have struck him very funny because he couldn't stop laughing even while brushing his teeth.

While he was brushing, I regulated the temperature of the shower water and by the time he was finished, the temperature was perfect. We stepped into the shower together and immediately crushed our bodies together in a bear hug. I took the soap in my hand and began to wash him all over, paying particular attention to his genitals and his ass. Robbie began to moan as I soaped his crack. As I did so, I slipped in one finger and was pleased to see that it went almost all the way in with no pain or resistance. I told you, he learns quickly and he started to do the same to me.

When I inserted a second finger, he flinched and I withdrew it at once. After a few seconds, I inserted the second finger again and it went in more readily. He did the same to me. We were face to face. Our throbbing dicks rubbed one on the other, and our fingers played inside our ass holes. Then I slipped in a third finger. Robbie gave a little cry of pain and did the same to me.

I did not add another finger but I started kneading his crack with the fingers already there, and began stretching him out to receive me. I had a bottle of baby oil in the shower. I separated from Robbie and turned him around. I lubed my cock generously with the baby oil and then reinserted the three fingers in Robbie's crack. This time my fingers were oily and met no resistance. I continued to stretch him and instructed him to put his hands on the wall and stick his butt out. When he was in position, I substituted my cock for my fingers as quickly as I could. I told you that I am not too big and I met very little resistance going in.

When I was totally in, I tried not to move, hard as that was. I let him get used to me and asked with some trepidation, "How do you feel? Does it hurt?" Robbie didn't answer. "Are you all right?" I asked again. Robbie made some sort of a guttural sound which frightened me, but I wasn't about to pull out.

"I thought last night was Nirvana, but now I'm in ecstasy. Fuck me, please," he whispered. "I feel like our bodies have fused together." I started to move slowly in and out of him. I came out as far as I could and then thrust in again. A couple of times I fell out of him and had to reinsert myself, but I went right in easily. That unmistakable feeling began to pervade my body and to grow strongly in my cock. "I'm cumming," I whispered in his ear.

"Cum inside me," was his response. Two more hard thrusts and I was doing the screaming, filling his guts with my juice.

"I can feel your stuff filling me up," Robbie whimpered. "It's more wonderful than I ever imagined." I pulled him to me and stayed in as long as possible, but the inevitable happened and my limp cock fell out. I immediately fell to my knees and began to lick Robbie's ass hole clean. I consumed as much of my own cum as dribbled out of him.

"When you sucked my ass hole," Robbie said later on, "that was the best part."

"Fuck me now," I begged as I handed him the bottle of baby oil. I must say I was a little worried because Robbie's cock was the biggest that had ever entered me. I needn't have been concerned. Not only did he prepare me as I had prepared him, but anticipating his larger size he worked four fingers in before inserting his cock. At his initial entry, it hurt like hell, but I pretended it didn't hurt at all and I urged him on. Soon he was all the way in and stayed perfectly still just as I had done, letting me get used to his size. I felt that someone had blown a balloon up my ass and it was wonderful.

I had previously had very few cocks up my ass and none had ever found my prostate. Robbie's monster was lying on it and when he began to stroke, his cock rubbed my prostate. The room began to spin. I was fainting and I didn't know how to tell him. If I did faint his huge cock held me tight so I couldn't fall to the floor. I felt another orgasm coming on and I spurted against the shower wall way before he let loose with his primeval scream, and squirted another huge load up my ass.

"How did you do that?" he asked after we had recovered somewhat. "How could you cum without my touching you?"

"Let's clean up and have breakfast and then I'll teach you about the birds and bees," I told him.

We decided to have breakfast out and then go to Robbie's place for a fresh change of clothes for him. Unfortunately none of my stuff fit him. At breakfast I explained to Robbie how I was able to cum without his stimulating me. I told him that his cock had rubbed against my prostate and that brought me to orgasm. My cock was smaller than his was, and apparently I hadn't given him the same pleasure. I promised that in the future we would experiment and I would find his sweet spot. To that he commented, "My life is getting sweeter and sweeter." He took my hand and squeezed it tightly.

Robbie's place was a furnished studio apartment. It was very cramped and very small. You couldn't even use the shower unless the bathroom door was open. The landlord provided a small refrigerator and a hot tray. The apartment had no oven.

"When is your lease up?" I asked

"I'm on a month to month."

"That requires a month's notice. If you give notice today you'll have to pay September's rent, and that's it. Move in with me today, Robbie. I know it's the right thing to do. I love you. I swear there will never be another guy in my life."

"Wow," he answered. "This is so quick."

"Not really, I've been in love with you since I met you in January. Besides I can't bear the thought of not sleeping with you every day for the rest of my life."

Robbie grabbed me and kissed me. He laid his cheek on mine and I could feel his tears. "It's a deal," he said, "for life."

He had one beat up old suit case which we packed for his immediate needs. That afternoon we came back with flat boxes which we put together and used to pack his stuff. He had so little that we didn't even use all the boxes. We were packed in less than an hour. We went down stairs to his landlord's apartment. Robbie gave him notice and a check for September's rent. I handed him my card to be used as a forwarding address.

"I'm sorry to see you go," the landlord said. "I don't often get such a good tenant like you." We left the building, and hailed a cab. The cabbie, Robbie, and I got his few boxes in the cab and Robbie gave his house key to the landlord. They shook hands and away we went for the short ride to my apartment. Again the cabbie helped us unload. As I was paying him and giving him a generous tip he looked at me and winked. "I hope you two will be as happy together as my partner and I." I wanted to grab and hug him, but he was off in a flash.

Robbie tried to pay for half the cab fare, but I wouldn't let him and we had our first 'fight.' Well I was glad that was out of the way.

It took no time to hang his stuff in my closet which was almost as empty as his had been. There was plenty of drawer space also. We laughed at how little we each had. We managed to survive only by washing our dirty clothes very often.

We marked the day Robbie moved in with me as our commitment day. Now thirty-five years later, we are getting ourselves ready to go to a big party we are throwing for all our friends to mark the event. It has been thirty-five glorious and happy years, especially since the very next time I fucked Robbie I found his prostate.

TORTURED SOULS

He was a married man. Very married. Thirty years worth of married. Three grown children, all married. No grandchildren yet, but the kids were still newly-weds.

He lay in bed every night, thinking, fantasizing about all his "might have beens." He lay on one side of the bed, as far to his end as possible, and his wife lay on the other, as far to her end as possible. Two people could sleep comfortably between them in the king size bed. They had not had sex in almost five years, and he pleasured himself often in the shower. She claimed that her arthritis was too painful and that he hurt her when he touched her. Every night when she went to sleep she pushed their pillows as far apart as she could, hoping that he would not accidently touch her at night.

His first fantasy every night was always the same. It wasn't a fantasy at all. It was a remembrance of a true experience in his life, and a lost opportunity.

He was in the navy, nineteen years old, still a virgin (that was his secret). One day one of his buddies asked him to go on liberty with him. He had a date, and the girl asked him to bring a friend for her girlfriend. His buddy assured him that it was a sure thing. He wanted so much to get laid, but his stomach was turned into a knot. He feared that he wouldn't be able to get it up. His sexual dreams were about men, not women. He knew what was going on with him, but he refused to admit the truth to himself. He believed that one day the right girl would come along and he would marry her and lead a 'normal' life.

He and his friend went to the restaurant where they were to meet the girls. He secretly hoped that they would get stood up, and in fact, the girls never came. They waited for more than an hour and finally left the restaurant. They were too young to drink in this state which had a minimum drinking age of twenty-one, so they waited outside a liquor store and asked a young customer to buy them a bottle of booze. The customer was glad to help out these two young and very handsome service men.

They took the bottle, safely tucked in a brown bag, and got a room at a nearby sleazy hotel. Once inside they opened the bottle and proceeded to chug-a-lug directly from the bottle. "Let's strip," his buddy said, "in case we get sick. We don't want to vomit all over our uniforms." They stripped down to their skivvies, and got a little drunker.

"I sure am horny tonight," his buddy said. "What a shame the girls stood us up. What do you say we whack off. I never can do it in the barracks with all those guys around."

"I wouldn't mind," he answered. "It's been a long time for me too."

They removed their skivvies. Both were hard as rocks. They began to jerk off and his buddy said. "Do me and I'll do you." By now he was quite drunk and happily agreed. He never did know exactly what happened next, but he was aware that out of curiosity they tasted each other's cocks, and then fucked each other using only their spit as a lubricant. Each sailor came in the other's ass.

He awoke in the morning and glanced at the dresser. The entire bottle of booze had been consumed. He knew what they had done the night before, but he had been too drunk to remember if he had enjoyed it. He wanted desperately to take his sleeping friend's cock in his hand and resume the activity of the night before, but he was scared shitless. If they were caught they would be dishonorably discharged. Their lives would be ruined.

Eventually they rose, freshened up and vacated the room. The incident was never spoken of again.

It wasn't until years later that he began to suspect that his buddy had seduced him, and that there never were any girls. He regretted not pursuing this event further and he called this incident one of his 'lost opportunities.' Lying in bed he would then fantasize that the two sailors resume making love in the morning, cold sober. They suck each other to orgasm and fuck each other over and over. The experience is wonderful and after that they go on liberty together as often as possible, and make man love until the navy separates them by assigning them elsewhere.

If he wasn't sleeping by the end of this fantasy, he began to remember other lost opportunities to be with a man. Many opportunities had presented themselves to him over the years. But always his fears had prevented him from acting upon them.

He could go as far back as his eighteenth year.

He was on a New York City subway at rush hour. He was squashed between several miserable commuters. The handsome young man facing him was in his early twenties. They smiled at each other. Suddenly he felt the man playing with his cock through his trousers. It felt good but he was scared to death. He said nothing and the man continued to play with him. At the next stop, he waited until the door was about to close. He pushed through the crowd and exited just as the doors closed behind him. The man had followed him, but was left staring though the glass. Their eyes met. The man's expression was sad. His eyes asked, "Why?" Or rather "Why not?"

Now his fantasy would begin. Instead of running away, he nods at the handsome stranger and begins to play with the man's cock. They stop playing as the crowd thins out. The stranger and he get out at the man's stop. He takes him to his apartment and introduces him to the joys of gay sex. The man sucks his cock and rims his ass. Sometimes he fucks the man and other times the man fucks him. After that first night they see each other often and when the time is right, he moves in with the young man and they become life partners. But alas! It was just another opportunity lost.

Still another lost opportunity often came to his mind. He was twenty-six and a newly-wed at the time:

A young college student worked as an intern in his office. He was pretty sure that the boy was gay, but he did not know any gay buzz words and had no real way of finding out. One day the boy mentioned that he was moving into an apartment of his own and needed to buy some wall décor. His wife was out of town visiting her parents. He told the boy that he had a few pieces of art in his basement that he was throwing out and invited him over after work to see if he could use any of it. The boy came over and chose a rather large landscape.

"This will be tough to hang without help," he said.

"No problem, I'll go over to your place and help you hang it," the man answered. "In the meantime, would you like a cup of coffee and a donut? We haven't had any dinner."

"That would be great," the young man said. So they sat around sipping coffee and eating donuts, when he steered the conversation to sex.

*"I envy you being a bachelor," he said. "Married sex sucks. My wife refuses to go down on me. Nobody ever has, and I want it so bad. **I'd give it to get it.**"*

There was no reaction at first and then the young man said, "I sure would like that myself."

"How about it then?" he asked.

"If you go first," the boy said.

"Ha, ha, very funny," he said, and they both laughed. The matter was dropped.

Then the fantasy would begin. "Sure, I'll go first," he says. He goes down on the boy and soon they are playing sixty-nine. They have wild passionate male sex all night. In the morning they go to work together. After the boy moves into his own apartment, they see each other as often as possible. They suck and fuck and give each other more pleasure than he ever could have dreamed.

And that's how he spent his nights, fantasizing, until he fell asleep. In the morning he would lock the bathroom door, and whack off while taking his morning shower.

The years passed and then a miracle occurred. He bought his first PC and went on line. He learned quickly how to find gay chat rooms and enter them. The thought of going to a gay bar had always been out of the question. The internet was a new opportunity, hopefully not a lost one. He hoped against hope to make contact with some gay man with whom he could at last have man sex. He prayed that his contact would live nearby and that they could meet and make love.

Most of the time, he didn't understand the repartee going on between the men in the chat room. He would have sent a message if he knew what to say. Basically, he was a voyeur at first, and then one evening it happened. He received an instant message from one of the inhabitants of the room. "Sixty Something in Ft Lauderdale."

> Hotguy1: *Hey man, your profile sounds just like mine.*

> Cutesr: *Really! I'll have to read it. Hold on a minute.* He found Hotguy1 and clicked on his profile. After reading the profile as fast as he could, he realized that he was chatting with another married, mature man. "Discretion required" was a dead give away.

> Cutesr: *You're right. We sound like clones. How old are you?*

> Hotguy1: *61*

> Cutesr: *Bingo, I'm 62 and that's a real number.*

> Hotguy1: *Are you as horny for a man as I am?*

Cutesr: *I don't know. How horny are you?*

They continued to chat back and forth for almost an hour, teasing each other, promising each other heaven knows what, and then...

Hotguy1: *Are you alone? Can you call me?*

Cutesr: *Yes, I'd like that. My wife is out playing bridge and won't be home for at least two more hours.*

Hotguy1: *I'm alone right now too. Call me.*

They exchanged telephone numbers, and they both signed off. His fingers shook as he pushed in Hotguy1's number, but then a voice answered. It was not what he expected. He expected some raspy old sounding voice, but the voice he got was sexy and kind sounding.

"Hello," he heard. "Is this Cutesr? Hi, this is Hotguy1, better known as Jim Spalding."

"My name is Ralph," he said. He wasn't quite ready to offer his surname. "Where do you live?" he asked.

"On the 300 block of Sycamore," Jim said. Unlike Ralph, Jim had no trouble offering personal information.

"I'm on Pine, just two streets over in the 200 block."

"Wow," Jim almost yelped. "It's a beautiful night. Why don't you take a walk toward me and I'll walk to you. We can meet at the corner of Reed and Third Avenue. I'm wearing jeans, sneakers, and a blue sport shirt."

"This is exciting," Ralph said. I'm wearing denim shorts, sneakers, and a red tee shirt. See you in five." He hung up and literally ran out of the house and up the street. His heart was pounding and he got a little dizzy from excitement.

Neither man was exactly running when they spotted each other, but they were approaching at a fast pace. They both liked what they saw. Jim was about five feet eleven inches with grey hair, and blue eyes. Ralph was about six feet with salt and pepper hair, and warm brown eyes. They were both well built, very little extra weight and no bellies.

They stood facing each other for a moment, not knowing the appropriate thing to do. Finally Jim extended his hand and they shook hands cordially. Ralph didn't want to let go, and held on way too long. Finally he let go and said, "Do you want to go to Morey's Diner on Second and have a cup of coffee with me? We can talk there."

"Yes, good idea."

They turned toward Second Avenue and started walking. At first they said nothing and then Ralph said, "This is my first time. Honest, I'm scared shitless."

"I only did this once before and it was a disaster," Jim commented. "I literally ran away from the guy. We never did have sex, so I go on fantasizing."

Ralph laughed. "We'll have to exchange and compare fantasies. I've given up believing that any of my dreams will ever come true."

"I know what you mean. Most of the time I feel like I'm tied to a stake and being tortured." Jim does look tortured, Ralph thought. I wonder if I look that way too. They had reached the restaurant and when they entered they both scanned the room. "There's a nice quiet table in the corner over there," Jim said, and they headed toward it.

They each ordered coffee and a toasted English muffin.

"I have fantasized being with a man for as long as I can remember," Jim started. "It only happened once when I was nineteen. I was so scared I couldn't enjoy it."

"Who was it with?"

"My cousin, who was visiting us. He was about twenty at the time. God, years later he married and had a slew of kids. One day he just disappeared, leaving his wife and kids. I can only guess why and where he went, but he told me that day that if anyone ever found out he was gay, he'd kill himself. I'd give anything to find him."

"Geez," I said, "and I thought that I was tortured. I've only had one experience myself. It was with a navy buddy. I was so drunk I can't remember if it was good or bad."

Jim looked around and could see that nobody was watching them. He put his hand on top of Ralph's, whose first impulse was to pull away. But he didn't and it really felt so good.

"If ever I wanted to lose my cherry," Jim said, "it would be with you. You're a good looking dude, man."

"Thanks. The feeling is mutual."

"Would you like to *get together?*" Jim asked Ralph pleadingly.

Ralph looked into Jim's eyes. Yes, he could definitely make love to this man. He was hungering even as he sipped his coffee. All he could do was nod.

"I've dreamt about this forever," Jim said. "I know just the place. It's a motel, not far from here, and they rent by the hour. I'm in real estate. I can always tell my wife that I'm showing property to someone. Just tell me when you can make it."

"Every Thursday my wife goes into Miami. She found a quack there who treats her for her arthritis. She lies on a bed for about four hours, while a slow drip of some shit enters her body. Frankly I think it's a placebo. Anyway she leaves about nine and makes a day of it. She gets home about 6:30. Do you think Thursday would be good for you? I'm retired. Any day is good for me."

"Thursday is perfect for me. It's tomorrow."

"Of course, I forgot. Could you pick up some condoms and lube, just in case?" Ralph asked.

"You bet. No problem. Now Ralph, do you think I might get your full name and address so I can pick you up at about 9:15 tomorrow morning?"

They both laughed at that and it pretty much concluded the coffee and muffins. Before leaving the restaurant they went to the bathroom together. Neither had to pee, but when they saw that they were alone, Jim pulled Ralph to him and kissed him full on the lips. At the same time they each grabbed the other's package and sighed. As they fondled each other, their lips parted and their tongues found each other.

"I've died and gone to heaven on the express," Ralph said.

"I'm in the same railroad car," Jim echoed.

When he got home, Ralph's wife was already there.

"Where were you?" she asked. "I was worried.

"It was such a lovely evening that I decided to take a walk."

"You could have left me a note," she said as she climbed the stairs, heading for the chaste bedroom.

The next morning Ralph did not whack off. He was saving it for Jim. He couldn't wait for his wife to leave. She seemed to be taking forever this morning and indeed she left about ten minutes later than usual. She was only gone a few minutes when Jim drove up. Ralph locked the house and bounded into Jim's car. When he sat down he leaned over and kissed Jim, who kissed him back. Then he put on his seat belt.

Ralph was a little worried about the check-in process, but he needn't have. Jim just signed one name, John Smith, in the book even though the two of them were standing there. The clerk didn't even look up. This was an every day occurrence for him.

The room was small, but it was so clean that it was antiseptic. You could smell the bleach in the worn out sheets, but neither of the men cared.

"Jim," Ralph said. "I've been fantasizing about having every opening in my body invaded by a fat cock so don't be afraid to ask me to do anything. I swear I won't say no to you."

"God Ralph, so have I. So have I."

"Let me tell you how my fantasies go," Jim said. "I undress with my lover and take him by the hand into the shower. We soap each other good and wash every part of our bodies. We tease each other in the shower, but don't cum. We save that for the bedroom."

"My fantasies usually start in bed, so you lead the way."

They undressed slowly never taking their eyes off the other. They both worked out and they had tight muscled bodies with very little fat. As the undressing progressed each could feel himself getting hard. When they were down to their briefs, Jim said, "Let me take that off for you." He approached Ralph, got down on his knees and pulled Ralph's briefs off with his teeth. In the process, he allowed his lips to brush Ralph's cock and balls. Ralph restrained himself from crying with joy. "Let me do that to you," he said.

When they were completely naked, they smiled at each other. They were both about seven inches of hard, uncut manhood. Their pricks were throbbing and bobbing up and down. They embraced each other and rubbed their cocks together as they each moaned softly.

In the shower, they soaped each other good. It was nothing for them to stroke the other's cock with a soapy palm, but when Jim started to insert a soapy finger up Frank's ass, Frank let him do it, but he whimpered.

Jim stopped. "Did I hurt you," He asked. "Why did you cry?"

"You didn't hurt me at all. I was crying for joy. Please let me do that to you."

They were working themselves into a frenzy, but finally they stopped, dried off and got into bed. In bed, they pressed their bodies together as their cocks ground hard, one against the other. They kissed passionately, but at this point each was afraid of taking the first step. Finally Jim rolled Ralph over and moved his kisses from Ralph's lips to his neck, and then down to his nipples, his navel, his inner thighs and then at last he began to suck Ralph's balls. All the while Ralph was making little whining sounds of pleasure. When Jim took

Ralph's cock in his mouth, he screamed, "Oh Jesus, what did I do to deserve this joy?"

After a few strokes of Jim's tongue along the underside of Ralph's cock, Ralph exploded into Jim's mouth. When he recovered enough to think about it, Ralph realized that Jim had swallowed all of his cum.

They lie side by side as Ralph caught his breath. "How did it taste?" he asked.

"Like honey, like ambrosia, like everything I ever dreamed of," Jim answered and now he began to cry. "I'm so happy," he sobbed.

Ralph leaned over and kissed Jim. Then his lips began a slow descent down Jim's body, suckling and teasing him. He teased him until Jim begged for mercy and then he swallowed Jim's prick down his throat, as far as he could get it. Jim came almost as fast as Ralph had, and Ralph swallowed every drop of Jim's cum.

Lying side by side, Jim asked, "When we get hard again, let's fuck each other."

"You bet," Ralph mumbled, and he cuddled up to Jim.

They gave up the room at 3 PM so that they would each be home in plenty of time. Before they said goodbye, they made plans for their next meeting. Of course, they would meet every Thursday, but Ralph's wife played bridge two evenings a week, and Jim's wife played canasta one night a week. Happily one of the bridge nights coincided, and they made plans to meet that night also.

Occasionally, they could break away and have lunch together, and on rare occasions, they managed a dinner. They were happy. Their tortured souls were eased at long last. But too much happiness has its consequences.

As they fell more and more in love, and as their need for each other grew exponentially, their marriages suffered.

Ralph's marriage deteriorated rapidly. His wife was a bit of a shrew, but in the past he had never answered her back. Suddenly he began to rebel against her ordering him around. She found fault with everything he did, and he facetiously asked if he ever did anything right. Their dinner dates were always with her friends and he could barely tolerate them. He started to balk at going out to dinner so often, and with people he disliked. She wept, telling him that he was ruining her social life, and she asked him what it was he wanted. She even began to ask him if he wanted to end the marriage. He never answered her, but he wanted to scream, "Yes, a thousand times, yes."

Jim's wife was a heavy drinker and an even heavier smoker. She reeked of tobacco and was usually so high, he couldn't bear to be in the same room with her. They fought constantly. He wanted desperately to leave her, but he was too loyal, and he felt so bad for her that he could not do such a thing.

One day he came home from work to find her lying in the hallway. Her lifestyle had finally caught up to her, and her heart had rebelled. At first he blamed himself. He should have been a better husband and been there more for her. After the initial shock of her sudden death, he realized that she had tried AA, rehab and therapy. He had supported her through all that, and he concluded that he would not blame himself ever again. Fortunately during his mourning period, Ralph was there for him, and the two became even closer if that was possible.

In the days that followed, Jim was always available to be with Ralph, but Ralph was still restricted. One day his wife spent hours on the phone. When she came out of their bedroom, she proclaimed triumphantly, "I have just filled up our calendar for every night for the next month. The next two evenings we are going to the same restaurant. I know you want mind because you love that restaurant."

Ralph remained silent. He stared at her in disbelief. The next Thursday when she left for Miami, he loaded his car with his essentials, and drove to Jim's house. He gave his wife everything he had in payment for his freedom. He even went back to work to support himself. At first Jim said that he was acting hastily and he should go home, but Ralph wouldn't budge.

There was much unpleasantness at first with lawyers and the divorce, but Ralph gave his wife everything she asked for, and the agony didn't last too long. The serenity, happiness and peace that prevailed in Jim's house, more than made up for the brief period of unpleasantness.

One evening they lay in bed, holding each other tight after having made love. Ralph said, "I had just begun to accept the fact that I would never make love to a man, and then you came into my life. I must have done something really wonderful for God to have rewarded me like this."

"It's funny. I feel the same way," Jim said. "I lived in hell, not only because of my wife's addictions, but because I couldn't express my love in the way God intended for me. Then you came along and changed my whole life. Thank you, sweetheart."

"No need for thanks. Just go on loving me, please," Ralph begged.

"For always," Jim assured him.

OLD ACQUAINTANCE

Hi y'all. My name is Bobby. I guess since I've reached the ripe old age of thirty, I should start asking people to call me Bob. I'm a good ole southern boy, who somehow found his way to The Big Apple, New York City. I practice law in this urban jungle and I love every minute of my life. It wasn't always so!

It's a big deal, moving from a small rural town in Georgia to the big city, but it had to be done and a guy's got to do what a guy's got to do. What I had to do was get out of town as soon as I possibly could. I went to New York University for my undergraduate work, and never returned to Georgia. From New York University I went directly to law school at Columbia University, and I started to work for a large law firm right after graduation. My visits to Georgia are very limited now, and I usually go there only around Christmas time.

It wasn't my parents I wanted to get away from. It was the town. Actually my parents are great. They paid my tuition through college and law school and let me know that it was an honor for them to do so, not a burden. They always stood behind me, even when I came out to them. They were always my biggest fans and supporters. I have to wonder why.

Life was awkward for me all through elementary, middle and high school. I was skinny, short, pimply and an all around nerd. But apparently my folks loved me enough to try to keep bolstering my self esteem. I was easy pickings for every bully in school. Then in high school it became obvious to a contingent of aggressive bullies that I was gay. I hate telling about the indignities I suffered from then on. As just a single example, the worst indignity I suffered was when five big guys stripped me in the school boys' room. They all pissed on me, and one shit on me, leaving me dirty and crying on the tile floor. Are you getting a clear picture of my need to exit town and quickly?

One of my tormenters was Mike Callahan. Here's where I must make a confession and tell you my life long secret. I fell in love with Mike in kindergarten. We became friends and played together every day after school. I could never tell him how much I loved him. We remained friends until we entered high school. By that time, Mike had become a hunk and I had only grown uglier.

In high school he wanted nothing to do with me and avoided me like the plague. I couldn't have him as a lover, of course, but my fantasies ran amok. I gleefully whacked off several times a day imagining that he was fucking me or sucking me or vice versa. Oh Mike, if you ever knew what joys I could bring to your beautiful body, you might have been kinder. I have always believed that I would take this secret to the grave.

Let me tell you what happened to me once I got out of Georgia. First of all, I made it my mission in life to lose my southern accent. Then without any effort at all, I grew to be six feet two inches tall. I worked out in the gym every chance I could get, and my tall frame became hard and ripped. Best of all, my acne disappeared. The bottom line is that I became a hunk. I even played football in college. I still fantasized every night that I was in bed with Mike, but little by little the Mike fantasy stopped, and I lived in the moment. Fuck you, Mike Callahan, and eat your heart out!

I was in my twelfth year away from Georgia, and in my fifth year in the law firm. One wonderful, wonderful morning, Mr. Becker, the senior partner in the firm, called me into his office. He had me sit comfortably on the other side of his desk. He started by reciting a litany of my accomplishments and let me know how valuable I was to the firm. Then he smiled, stuck out his hand and told me that I was being offered a junior partnership. How quickly I advanced to senior partner was all up to me. Of course I thanked him profusely. Then he did something very atypical for him. When I stood up to leave, he stood up too. He threw his arms around me and gave me a bear hug. That lasted a moment and then we were all business again.

I immediately called my parents. They were thrilled for me and kept telling me how proud they were of my accomplishments. It was all I could do to get them off the phone. Then I called my very best friend, Matt Finch. His cell phone took my message and he called me back in about twenty minutes. Matt teaches drama at the City College of New York, and it seems he's always in class when I call. Matt said that my news called for a celebration *ON HIM*, and we agreed to meet at our favorite watering hole at 9 PM. Unfortunately, he had a rehearsal of a Tennessee Williams play that his drama students were preparing for presentation. He hoped he could make it by 9, or 9:30 at the latest, he promised.

Let me digress a moment and tell you about Matt. I met Matt in my first class on my first day at NYU. I was still the nerdy hick from Georgia and Matt was a bit of an outcast himself. He stood about 5'9" tall and was a good fifteen pounds overweight, but not fat. He was far from handsome, but he wasn't ugly either. What he lacked in physical appearance he made up in personality. I myself never had that ability. His face bore a perpetual smile which formed the cutest dimples. He was upbeat and brought everyone around him up to his level. He was sharp and witty and became popular even though he had been shunned in high school just as I had been. I became more popular just by associating with him.

We both lingered a moment after class that first day. I know for sure we recognized each other as kindred outcast souls. We introduced each other and simply said, "See ya tomorrow." It was a very unpromising beginning.

Matt and I spoke to each other for a few minutes every day before and after class for about the first five weeks. Then we would go our separate ways. Finally one day, I screwed up my courage and asked Matt if he would like to have a drink with me this evening and maybe a burger at Burger King. His eyes just illuminated and I could see the light of his joy diffuse through his whole body. At that moment this chubby little guy looked as cute as any guy I had ever fantasized about. "Easy Bob," I had to tell myself. "He's straight!"

From that day on, we saw a lot of each other. We had our fast food dinners together almost every night; had an occasional drink at a local pub; studied together in the school library; and then returned to our separate dorm rooms.

After the first semester my room mate dropped out of school and Matt was able to move in with me. It was a great move for both of us because we had become best friends. We got to see each other naked since we both slept in the buff. He was nothing special. If anything, he was a little below average. But I got to see his morning woodies and realized that he grew substantially to a very respectable size. I was at least half again larger than he and we joked about it a lot. By the way we were both circumcised. What I loved most about him were his love handles. I began to fantasize making love to Matt and squeezing his love handles as I shot my load. It was an effort to force myself to give up thinking that way about him.

One fateful day Matt told me that he had been invited to a friend's birthday party and he couldn't have dinner with me that night. I myself could not get over how lost I felt. I asked Matt if there was any chance I could tag along, and he said that it would not be possible this time. I asked why, and he said that he would tell me someday, but not tonight.

After Matt left I was feeling pretty lonely. At this time I had not yet had any sexual experiences with a male or a female for that matter. Through the grapevine I had heard about a gay bar not too far from the university. At this point I didn't care if I ran into any students I knew. I was ready to come out and lose my virginity. I dressed in what I thought was appropriate attire for a gay bar, a tee shirt with cut off sleeves, a pair of tight jeans and flip flops. I put on a stylish leather jacket, and off I went to The University Club.

The place was dimly lit and I had to stand just inside the entrance for a while until my eyes became accustomed to the dark. I finally spotted what appeared to be the bar and I meandered over to it. At this point in my life I was almost full grown. I had begun to play football, and I was not a bean pole any more. I still had acne and I still wore glasses. Contacts were in my future. I found a seat at the bar and ordered a gin and tonic. The bartender carded me. Nobody was pushing through the crowd trying to meet me so I sat quietly by myself looking around and getting a sense of New York's "gay scene."

After awhile I heard a lot of laughter coming from a large table not too far from the bar. I looked over and saw about ten guys seated around the table. One of them was opening gifts. Obviously it was a birthday party, and all the gifts were gags. With each opening they all burst into laughter. After opening each gift, the birthday boy got up and kissed the gift's giver.

The fifth gift he opened turned out to be an oversized dildo. It was at least a foot long and as wide around as a good size salami. Everyone at the table was hysterical and I laughed too. The birthday boy got up and walked over to the friend who had given him the dildo and my heart stopped beating. It was Matt.

Dear sweet Matt. Dear unattractive Matt. Dear man, who had grown to mean so much to me, Matt was gay. I realized that he thought I was straight, and that's why he didn't want me tagging along this evening. I panicked and ran from the bar and straight back to our room. I was in a dilemma. Should I tell him that I knew or should I wait for him to come out to me? Should I come out to him?

I ran to the showers and let the hot water cleanse my body as if my mind could be cleansed also, and I would somehow know what to do. When Matt came home, just a wee bit tipsy, I said and did nothing, and life continued as it had. We were still just good friends.

I could not live much longer knowing he was gay, wanting him, and doing nothing about it. Every night as he lay snoring lightly in the bed across the room from me, I began to fantasize making love to him. My cock would rise to the occasion and as silently as possible, I whacked off, catching my jism in some paper toweling I had put under my pillow. If Matt ever jacked off, I was unaware of it. I never heard him or caught him at it. I shouldn't be surprised. I was being just as cautious.

One night madness came over me. I heard his near quiet snoring, and knew he was asleep. I got out of bed and crept cautiously into his bed. There was hardly room for both of us. I nestled against him like two spoons in a drawer. My hard cock pressed against his naked ass and my arm went around him. I took this opportunity to squeeze his adorable love handles ever so lightly. Then I reached further down and wrapped my hand around his limp cock. I thought he was still asleep but I heard him murmur, "Thank you, Lord."

We both fell asleep that way and never even made love that night, but oh, the next morning we consummated our love and I have never looked back since. We missed our morning classes in favor of sucking and fucking until we were so exhausted we missed our afternoon classes as well. Thinking back on it now, I am grateful that my first time was with such a caring and thoughtful lover as my Matt.

As long as I am in a confessing mood, I must confess that the first couple of times I made love to Matt, I fantasized that he was Mike Callahan. As my love for Matt grew exponentially, that fantasy disappeared forever.

The night of my promotion, I changed into my "bar attire" and started out for The University Club. Matt and I had agreed to meet at the bar so when I got there I knew immediately that I had arrived first. If I knew Matt, and I knew him well, I would be lucky if he showed up before 10:30. Things were so different for me now at the Club. Friends kept coming over to give me a kiss or a hug or both and to ask me how I was doing.

I headed for the bar, and I tried to save the seat next to me for Matt. Good looking guys kept coming over trying to put the make on me, but I told them all to buzz off. I was waiting for a friend. In the darkened room, I couldn't see any of them until they actually sat down next to me. Then I heard a voice say, "Hey handsome, are you alone?"

My brain began to clang. I knew that voice, knew it well, right down to the southern drawl, but I couldn't place it. I looked up and right into the eyes of Mike Callahan. I would know him anywhere. He was as handsome as ever. His blue eyes were piercing right through my heart, which was being challenged to continue beating.

"Yes, I'm alone," I said, and he sat down in the seat I was holding for Matt.

"Can I buy you a drink?" he offered me.

"Not yet," I answered. "I'm still nursing this one. You don't recognize me do you?" I asked.

"No. Should I? Did we ever get together?"

"Hardly," I answered and began to laugh. "Think back to high school. Do you remember Bobby Rogers?"

"A sneer came across Mike's face. "Sure I do," he said. "What an ugly little nerd. Did you know him too?"

"Pretty well," I answered. "You're talking to him." I wish I could have photographed the look on Mike's face at that moment.

"I don't believe it," he finally managed to say. "When I knew you in high school you were skinny and pimply faced. Now you look like a Greek God. You are so hot, man. The transition is remarkable."

"I know," I answered. "I'm at least a foot taller. In college I started exercising and I lived on protein diets. You didn't know me in college, but I played football there." Mike looked at me in astonished awe.

"Why did you stop being my friend back then?" I asked. "I really had the hots for you."

"I must have been a major jerk," Mike answered. "You know there's a lot of peer pressure in high school. If I was to remain with *the in group*, there was no room for you." He said that as if it was a universal truth.

"Hey, that's all water under the bridge," I declared. "Let's talk about now."

"You grew up to be one hot dude, Bobby," Mike said. Then with a wink of his eye he added. "I saw your tiny weenie in the boys' room, but I'd sure like to see that cock of yours now."

"There's an empty table over there. Let's grab it," I said, "then you can reach under the table and feel for yourself, handsome. Nobody will see and if they did, they wouldn't care, not in this joint anyway." We sat down at the table and Mike lost no time in taking me up on my offer. When he managed to get my cock out through my fly it was hard and throbbing with desire. I hated myself for it, but I realized that I was still hot for Mike.

Mike's eyes got a look of pleading in them, and he said, "Let's go someplace where we can do this right."

"My cock is so hard, I'll never be able to stand up," I replied. "Let's just sit here for awhile and talk a bit. Tell me what you would like us to do together, handsome."

Mike giggled. Under the table he continued to stroke my exposed cock.

"That's nice," I said, "but I don't want to start something here in a public place. I still want to know what you would like us to do."

Mike giggled again. The question had made him very self conscious, but he cleared his throat and said, "I want us to suck each other and fuck each other, but not in ordinary ways. I want us to find new and innovative ways to do it. Oh Bobby, you are the hottest guy I have ever seen. I can't wait for us to fuck our brains out together. I thank the gods that we ran into each other again. Please let's get out of here before I explode."

"Don't be so impatient. The night is young," I said.

"I'll try to be patient, but it's going to be hard," Mike replied.

Just then Matt approached the table and called out to me. I jumped up and embraced him. Mike was confused and appalled. The guy I kissed was overweight by at least twenty pounds, and worst of all, he was balding. His face was very plain, and he had a couple of zits on his forehead. He had obviously come from work because he was wearing a tie. For some reason it irked Mike that the man seemed to be successful. Mike wondered why the hell a hot looking guy like me was being so nice to this loser. He sat back and waited for me to get rid of him. He hoped I would fail to introduce him to this freak.

I looked at Mike with a sly smile and said, "I'd like you to meet my partner, Matt. I love him for every bit of the man he is, and for the beauty that is inside of him. I couldn't exist without this man. I hope someday you can learn to look inside a man's soul to find his beauty, and not just judge him by his physical appearance."

Mike's jaw dropped down. He actually said, "No way! You're pulling my leg."

In answer to that insult, Matt and I walked away from Mike, heading for a group of men that Mike had always considered to be an elite bunch of hunks. He had been trying to crash their enclave forever, but they didn't seem to want to let him in. He watched as everyone in the group embraced Matt and me. He kept his eyes on us all evening and his whole body cringed when the entire group raised their champagne glasses to toast me on my promotion and my success.

I would like to think that Mike learned a lesson that night and that he will someday be able to find true love. I tell you this in all sincerity. I wish him no ill will.

ABOUT THE AUTHOR

Hank Brooks was born in Brooklyn, NY and lived most of his adult life in and around the New York City area.

He is very active in SAGE, a senior advocacy group for gay men and women.

He has three children and five grandsons. He is a retired CPA, and now lives with his partner, Leo, in Coconut Creek, Florida.